C0046 15783
JONES MYSTERY
GLASGOW
GHOUL
D0654307

Also by Joan Lennon and published by Catnip
in our *Slightly Jones Mysteries* series:

The Case of the London Dragonfish

For younger readers in our *Tales from the Keep* series:

The Ferret Princess
Wag and the King
The Mucker's Tale

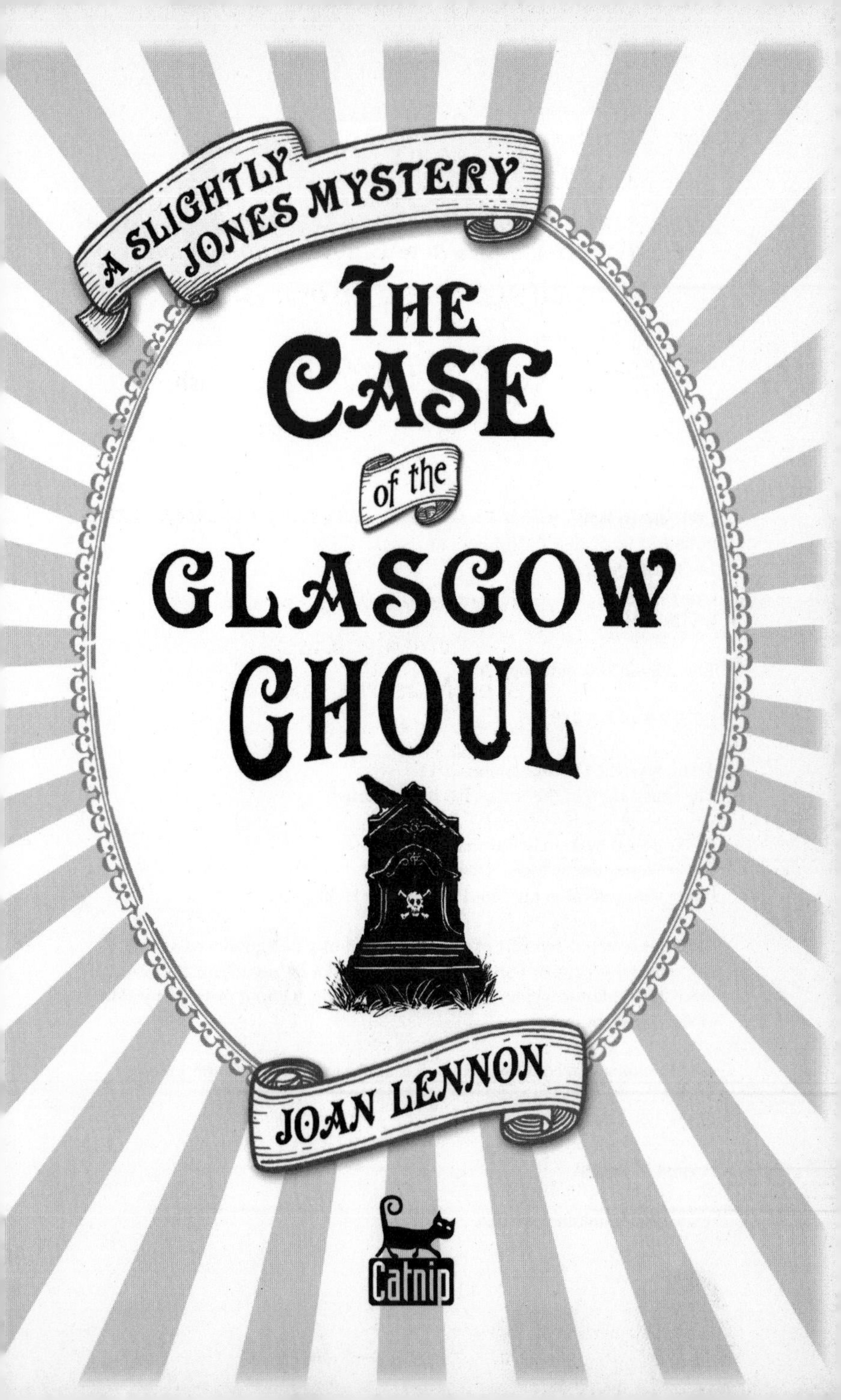
A SLIGHTLY JONES MYSTERY
THE CASE
of the
GLASGOW
GHOUL
JOAN LENNON
Catnip

CATNIP BOOKS
Published by Catnip Publishing Ltd
14 Greville Street
London
EC1N 8SB

This edition first published 2011

1 3 5 7 9 10 8 6 4 2

Cover design by Mandy Norman
Cover illustration by Shane Clester
Inside illustrations on pp. 156–157 by Jamie Heitler

A CIP catalogue record for this book is available from the British Library.

ISBN 978-1-84647-114-8

Printed in Poland

www.catnippublishing.co.uk

Everybody's heard of Florence Nightingale
and David Livingstone. These books are dedicated
to the Victorian heroes and heroines
who aren't quite so famous!

This one is for
Joseph Lister – Medical Pioneer

CONTENTS

The Snatched Revenge 9
A New Case 15
London Particular 23
On to the Second City of the Empire . 39
Night-time Prowlers and Daytime Ducks 53
Mr John's Cunning Plan 71
Into the Night! 83
House of the Dead 97
The Intruders 117
Seeing Ghosts Can Change Your Life . 131
Slightly's Big Idea 137
Three Letters 145
Fascinating Facts 153

Chapter One:

The Snatched Revenge

Jimmy was feeling proud and pleased. His uncle Duncan, the best resurrection man in all of Glasgow, had been saying for years, 'As soon as the lad's strong enough to dig up a corpse on a rainy night and carry half its weight as far as the cart, then I'll take him on.'

Well, Jimmy had grown a lot lately.

'I'm strong enough now, Uncle Dunc,' he'd said.

'Right you are then, Jimmy,' said his uncle. 'Meet me at the Glasgow Royal Infirmary tonight.

Twelve midnight. On the dot.'

'We're going to snatch bodies from the hospital?!' asked Jimmy, puzzled – and then he yelped, 'OW!'

Uncle Duncan was quick with his fists.

'Eyes open, mouth shut and a clout round the lughole for every daft question,' he said cheerfully. 'That's the way to learn.'

Jimmy rubbed his ear and resolved to ask no more questions. He *wanted* to learn, so he could become the best resurrection man in the fine city of Glasgow, just like his uncle. That was his ambition.

He remembered the very first time he'd asked Uncle Duncan about his work. Jimmy was still a little boy then. There'd been some trouble when a doctor refused to pay the full price for the corpse Uncle Duncan had brought him – just because he said it wasn't properly fresh!

'And he knows I can't report him to the police without getting into trouble myself,' his uncle had grumbled to Jimmy's mum. 'But then I said I'd never supply him again – and I'd make sure no other resurrectionist did either – well, then he *had* to pay up, didn't he?'

'Those doctors – they need you, don't they, Uncle Dunc?' the much younger Jimmy had asked.

'That's right, lad. Without bodysnatchers they'd

have hardly anybody to cut up and look into and study. And then suppose you were to, I don't know, go into the new Underground tunnel they're building and a wall collapsed on you and all your inside bits spewed out – how would the doctors know what order to put them back in? You could end up all wrong. Just think of that!'

Jimmy did think of it, and was impressed.

'So you're, like, a hero then, aren't you, Uncle Dunc?'

That, it would seem, was not a daft question, because instead of a clip on the ear, he'd got a shiny penny.

And now the day – well, the night, really – had come at last for Jimmy to start being a hero too.

They picked up the Infirmary cart from behind the hospital. At the nearby cemetery – a place so vast they called it the Necropolis, the City of the Dead – the gatekeeper had been bribed in advance, and was carefully looking the other way as Jimmy and his uncle trundled past. Once through the gate and over the bridge, they laboured up the hill, surrounded on every side by strange dark shapes. Jimmy was filled with admiration at how expertly his uncle found his way, following first one path and then another through the maze of monuments, funeral statues, humble tombstones and elaborate mausoleums as big as houses.

Then Uncle Duncan stopped.

'Here we are.'

He handed Jimmy a spade and opened the door of the dark lantern. The light fell on a mound of recently turned earth. 'There's a lovely fresh grave for you, my boy. Now let's see just how good you are.'

Jimmy started digging right away. He dug with enthusiasm. This was it – the beginning of his career as a hero! It wasn't even very hard, though he did have a funny feeling . . . a creepy sort of shiver between his shoulders . . . as if someone were watching him . . .

Jimmy looked round and the shovel dropped from his hands.

'Keep going, boy, you're not near done,' grunted his uncle, but Jimmy didn't move.

'Uncle Dunc?' he quavered.

'What?'

'Do you believe in ghosts?'

'That's a daft question.' Uncle Duncan gave a weary sigh. 'Come over here so I can clout you.'

No reaction.

'I *said* get over here,' repeated Uncle Duncan. In the dim light of the lantern, the expression on the boy's face was starting to make him uncomfortable.

‘W-what are you looking at?’

Slowly he turned round and his words died away in a terrified gargle.

Something ghastly and sepulchral was drifting towards them, strange, pale, draped in a shroud, with wide white wings held out to either side. It seemed not to be touching the ground as it moved. It had no face . . .

And yet it spoke.

‘Begone,’ they heard it whisper, its voice hoarse and low as if rusty from disuse. ‘Begone and never come again. Never come again, disturbers of my rest.’

Its last words were louder, hissing, threatening, but still neither Jimmy nor his uncle were able to move. Terror had rooted them to the ground like two new statues, until . . .

. . . the ghoul screamed.

Then the bodysnatchers scattered down the hillside on legs they could barely control, past astonished stone angels and black mausoleum doors, which gaped and beckoned them in. If one of the runners had fallen it was doubtful the other would have even paused to help, so powerful was their need to be somewhere – anywhere! – else.

Then, as the noise of their flight died away, another sound was heard amongst the graves.

A sound more chilling somehow than even the spectral scream.

The sound of ghostly laughter . . .

Chapter Two:
A New Case

Meanwhile, four hundred miles southeast, in London, Slightly Jones twisted and turned, whimpering. She was surrounded by hungry, inescapable flames – the heat was unbearable – already her hands were starting to melt, dripping onto the floor like candle wax – but even worse than the fire, there was something moving towards her, pale, faceless, ghastly . . . *a ghost!* She screamed but her voice made no sound. She tried to run but something was wrong with her legs – the ghoul was calling to her now, louder and louder –

'Slightly! Open your eyes! Slightly!'

It's trying to trick me! she thought, but then, without meaning to, she did open her eyes, and saw . . . Granny! Slightly was in her own room, in her own bed. Outside her attic window the sky was dark. It was still only the middle of the night.

But the flames had seemed so real . . .

'Just another nightmare,' Granny was saying, as she lit the candle. 'It's all over now. In the meantime, the thing to do is direct your attention somewhere else. Now, that was an extremely interesting story Mr John Gentler had to tell us, wasn't it! There's plenty there to keep your detective's brain busy!'

As always, Granny was right. Strange thefts, rumours of a one-legged man and an exotic beast, hints of the supernatural . . . it was more than just interesting – it was the kind of story to make a detective as great as Mr Sherlock Holmes smile with excitement and anticipation! And here it was, falling right into the lap of Slightly Jones, detective-in-training!

Slightly knew she didn't *look* like a detective – not at all, not a whit, not even a little bit. She was spindly. And freckly. And pointy-faced. Not to mention the fact that she had curly, unruly, utterly red hair.

How she hated her hair.

I look like a ginger ferret, she told herself with a disgusted squirm.

'Here's your notebook,' said Granny. 'And this very fine propelling pencil which, if I'm not much mistaken, your favourite granny gave you on your last birthday.'

'You're *never* mistaken,' said Slightly with a cheeky smile.

'And you can write *that* in any book you choose,' said Granny firmly. 'Goodnight!'

'Goodnight,' said Slightly, snuggling down a little and waving the pencil as her door closed.

This is what detectives do, she thought to herself. *They lay out their clues and solve their mysteries when all the rest of the world is fast asleep. Well, all the world except Mr Thurgood.*

Her friend, their lodger Mr Thurgood, was an insomniac novelist and did most of his writing at night. It was a comforting thought that he was probably propped up in bed in his own room just downstairs, not sleeping too.

Slightly opened her notebook at the first page, where she had written, in her best copperplate hand:

This book belongs to:
Detective Slightly Jones

Limpopo House
London
England
Great Britain
The World
The Solar System
The Universe

And then, at the bottom of the page, with little stars to decorate them, the words: Long Live Queen Victoria!

Here Slightly paused and wondered – not for the first time! – why Granny had called her house Limpopo, a place she knew to be far away in South Africa. She was sure it would be a story well worth hearing, but Granny wouldn't tell it. *It's The Case of the Mystifying Name,* she thought, but she didn't write that down. Granny's mysterious past would probably need a whole new notebook to itself.

To be accurate, Granny Tonic wasn't really her granny at all. She was Slightly's mother's aunt and so *her* great-aunt, but Slightly had always called her Granny because everybody else did. Limpopo House became her home when she was a baby, when her parents died. Since then, Slightly's family had been Granny and her lodgers.

There was Mr Earnest Thurgood, who combined his job as nightwatchman at the Natural History Museum with writing what would one day be an exceptionally successful series of detective stories. There was Miss Sally Forth, who (in spite of being annoyingly fluttery) probably knew more languages than anyone else in the entire world, and Mr Reginald Westerly, the artist and owner of a truly splendid moustache. And there was Mr Malcolm Gentler. Mr Malcolm could play any instrument ever invented. He made his living playing in theatre orchestras, but his real life's work was writing songs – the best songs Slightly had ever heard.

And now there was Mr Malcolm's brother.

Turning to a fresh page in her notebook she wrote: *The Remarkable Story of Mr Malcolm's Brother from Scotland.*

Then she shut her eyes, remembering . . .

Mr John Gentler had arrived unexpectedly just last evening to visit his brother, and had ended up telling them all his troubles. Granny's kitchen was like that. People felt safe there and, well, things just came out.

Sometimes they came out in a bit of a jumble, however. Mr John had been quite agitated, running his hands through his hair as he talked. He was telling them about the robberies from his museum

– a whole string of them – which had completely bewildered the trustees and the police.

'We have doubled the locks, hired more nightwatchmen, installed the latest alarm system, tried to safeguard the exhibits in every way we can think of, and still the thefts continue.' Mr John sounded positively desperate. 'No one knows who is doing them, or how! Some of the trustees at the Museum favour the idea of a one-legged man and an exotic beast, while others have been affected by the spate of wild stories about ghosts and the walking dead, and even I have . . .' He paused suddenly. 'Excuse me, I fear I have said too much and too unclearly! I have no wish to alarm . . .' and he looked at Slightly.

'Oh, I'm not a bit afraid,' she assured him, 'though I do have some questions!' She was just about to start interrogating their guest when Granny had intervened.

'It is quite late and I can see you're tired,' she had said, politely but firmly as well. 'Perhaps you would visit us again when we have all rested?'

Mr John stood up immediately.

'You are very kind,' he said with a bow. 'I am staying at the Euston and Victoria Hotel, but I will, with your kind permission, return tomorrow at any time that is acceptable.'

‘Please join us for breakfast,’ said Granny. ‘I always think it is wisest to strike while the toast is hot. Slightly, say goodnight.’

‘Oh, please, I’m not –’ began Slightly, but one look at Granny’s face told her this was not an argument she was likely to win.

I’ll go to bed but I know I won’t sleep, she grumbled to herself, stomping up the first flight of stairs. Then, just as she came to the landing she heard Mr Malcolm saying, ‘I’ll see my brother out’ and the two men came into the entrance hall. Looking down through the railings, Slightly could see them standing together by the front door as Mr John buttoned his coat.

For a whole second, Slightly hesitated. There was a struggle in her mind between the good manners Granny had taught her and the things that every detective must do in order to gather clues and solve a case. According to The Ways of Granny, eavesdropping was bad. According to The Ways of Detecting, eavesdropping was an excellent means of finding things out.

The Ways of Detecting won.

She listened hard as Mr Malcolm said in a low voice, ‘What is it, John? It’s not just the robberies, is it? What else are you upset about?’

Mr John shook his head. ‘I’m sorry. It’s just that

. . . do you remember what it was like when . . . when Father used to punish us?'

'Do I remember?! I only stopped sleepwalking and having bad dreams when I came here!' said Mr Malcolm sadly. 'Why do you ask? Have *you* been troubled by night terrors lately?'

'No. Yes. But not dreams of Father, his anger and his cane. This has been much more real. It's Jenny!' And Mr John grabbed his brother by the sleeve. 'I've *seen* her! She . . . she's come back!'

'From the dead?!'

Slightly had to clamp her hands over her mouth to keep from squeaking out loud.

'I know, I know,' Mr John was saying. 'It's impossible. And yet I swear, Malcolm, it's true. I saw her! She spoke to me! I . . . she . . . I . . .' His voice cracked. It was clear to Slightly that he was struggling with some great emotion.

'Don't upset yourself, John. Rest now, and we'll talk later.' Mr Malcolm patted his brother's shoulder.

Unseen above, Slightly gnawed on her knuckles in frustration.

The two brothers shook hands, Mr John left, and Slightly was forced to go to her bed with no way of getting answers to her questions till the next morning . . .

Chapter Three:
London Particular

Slightly opened her eyes to find the candle guttered, the delicious smell of frying bacon drifting up to her bedroom and the sound of a voice downstairs.

'I was lucky to get here at all!'

It was Mr John, speaking to Granny as he came through the front door again. It was morning. Slightly leaped out of bed and started to throw on her clothes any which way.

Mr John's words filled her with excitement. *Lucky to get here,* she thought eagerly. *The plot thickens!*

Perhaps he was pursued by knife-bearing strangers, intent on robbery – no, kidnapping! – they were trying to kidnap him and he only just escaped . . .

For a moment she had trouble thinking of a reason anyone would *want* to kidnap Mr Malcolm's brother, but of course if she'd been on the scene some clue would have revealed all.

'It's this filthy fog!' Mr John said next.

Ah. Not kidnappers then, thought Slightly. She couldn't help feeling a little disappointed. Fog was horrible, but not really very thrilling. As she scurried down the last flight of stairs she was just in time to see a great swathe of the stuff oozing into the hallway as Granny shut the door.

It was a real London Particular.

A London Particular was not *just* a fog. It was much, much worse. It was a dingy yellow thickness that filled the air, billowing up against the windows and fingering the doors. Humans and animals coughed and choked. The streetlamps stayed lit all day, pinpricks of orange that only managed to illuminate little circles in the blur. Slightly had heard many a tale of a Londoner being bewildered in their own city, and little street boys cobbled together pitch torches to earn some pennies lighting the way of those who could afford them.

'I walked,' Mr John was saying. 'It didn't seem safe to trust myself to a cab driver who could see no better than I could myself. I hired a lad with a torch – though how *he* knew the way I'll never know!'

'Good morning, Mr John!' Slightly greeted him, trying not to sound like a guilty eavesdropper.

'Good morning to you, young miss, though if you'd been outdoors as I have you'll know it is probably a vain wish! This is truly not a day for man nor beast.'

'Come into the kitchen, Mr John,' said Granny. 'You'll soon warm up.'

The lodgers of Limpopo House were already there.

'I do hope you'll excuse our breakfast informality, Mr John,' twittered Miss Forth anxiously, as their guest sat down at the kitchen table.

Slightly wished Miss Forth would stop being so *fussy*! They ate *all* their meals in the kitchen now that Mr Westerly was living in what used to be the dining room. Good light is hugely important to an artist, and so it was the best possible room for him to occupy. Slightly knew that Miss Forth didn't disagree – it was just that she worried whether other people might think it wasn't entirely *respectable*, eating in the kitchen. (Her elderly cat Cleopatra, on the other hand, much preferred the arrangement, since it meant she could get out into the back garden quickly when the need arose. But then cats have never been greatly concerned with the opinions of others.)

'I will let you in on a secret, Miss Forth,' said Mr John solemnly. 'When I am in my Glasgow house I always wish I *could* eat in the kitchen. But my housekeeper, Mrs Mull, won't let me. She insists on trudging back and forth across the whole empty house, just to serve me, and by the time she arrives, my eggs and bacon have entirely congealed.'

'Do you have a very large house, Mr John?' asked Granny politely.

Who cares about his house – let's hear about the crime! exclaimed Slightly impatiently inside her head. *Or better yet, tell us about that ghost!*

But of course Mr John didn't hear her, and answered Granny's question instead. 'Very large and very ugly,' he said. 'A dreary mausoleum of a house, where I rattle about like a pea in a jar, from one year's end to the next without any of the good company you have here!' And he raised his teacup in a toast to Granny who smiled, and was just about to fill it up for him when the back door slammed.

'That's it!'

Everyone whipped round in surprise.

'That's it – he's the music man's brother, sure as I'm breathin'!'

Someone was standing by the back door holding a doused torch, with a big grin on his dirty face and fog-drops dripping off his mud-coloured hair.

'Matthew Bone!' cried Granny and the lodgers in delight.

'Matthew Bone,' muttered Slightly with a lot less enthusiasm. (She found a little of Matthew went a very long way. Of course all detectives had contacts in the criminal underworld, but Slightly wished her contact could be *anybody* but Matthew Bone.)

'That's my name,' Matthew was saying, 'but don't spread it about – that don't pay in my line of work. Still, seeing as how you're near enough family, I'll make you a present of it! Oh, and speaking of presents, I suppose I better return these . . .'

'What the devil?!' spluttered Mr John. Slightly couldn't help grinning at the look of outrage on Mr John's face as, with a cheeky bow and a flourish, Matthew produced a fine silk handkerchief and a pocket watch and laid them on the kitchen table. 'Where did you get those?'

'Never noticed a thing, did you?' said Matthew smugly.

'Matthew is, I regret to say, a pickpocket,'

explained Granny. 'He also, on occasion, housebreaks and lock-picks.'

'Don't stint yourself, missus – I'm the best in all London at *anything* in the robbery game!' said Matthew.

As long as that includes boasting, grumbled Slightly silently. But then she gave herself a shake. She knew she was being shabby and petty-minded. *And that is not the way a good detective behaves. Matthew* does *have criminal expertise . . .*

'Perhaps we should ask Matthew's thoughts on the thef –' she began, but Mr John immediately held up a warning hand and shook his head at her.

'I don't think we need burden the young man with my little problem, Miss Slightly. I find in business, it's usually least said, soonest mended.'

Slightly could feel her temper starting to boil up.

But Matthew just shrugged. 'You're not a patch on your brother, mate,' he said rudely. 'I'm off – Matthew Bone can tell when he's not wanted!'

And before anyone could disagree, he was gone again, with nothing but a few tendrils of yellow fog left behind as the door shut.

Slightly turned on Mr John. 'But Matthew could have helped you with the robberies!' she exclaimed indignantly.

Mr John stroked his chin. 'Ask a thief how to catch a thief? Interesting idea . . . but I don't think my museum has sunk quite *that* low yet.'

Before she could reply – and it was obvious from the expression on her face that it was not going to be a *polite* reply – Granny distracted Mr John with more tea, and Mr Malcolm drew the fuming Slightly to one side.

'Don't be angry with my brother,' he said softly. 'He has been very much alone and business doesn't breed trust. Certainly our father was a deeply suspicious man. Matthew was just a step too far.'

Slightly unclenched her fists. 'All right, I'll try,' she said grudgingly. 'But I'm glad *you're* the Gentler brother who lives with me, and not him!'

'Me too!' whispered Mr Malcolm.

'I fear I may have been unclear at our previous meeting,' Mr John was saying. 'I was weary from the journey and hadn't my wits about me. I'd like to make a more business-like job of it this morning.'

Mr Malcolm rolled his eyes at Slightly, who suppressed a giggle.

Mr John didn't appear to notice. 'As I mentioned last night, I am a trustee of the Hunterian Museum, the first and the finest of Glasgow's museums. Our reputation is precious to me – and so are the exhibits!

Who is stealing them? How are they managing it? No one is able to solve the mystery.'

'We've heard nothing about this in the newspapers, have we?' Slightly looked at Mr Westerly, who often read the papers aloud to them all. The only news from Glasgow that she could remember were some tantalisingly short mentions of unnamed citizens swearing they'd seen ghosts in a graveyard. Nothing to do with museums at all.

'So far we've managed to keep our losses a secret,' said Mr John. 'Our reputation would be in tatters if it got out, and the results of *that* could be very harmful indeed. My present trip to London is a case in point. I am here to negotiate the gift of a valuable sacrificial knife brought back by Captain Cook from his voyages in the South Pacific. We at the Hunterian very much wish to have this prestigious artefact for our collection, but if it were known that our security is being breached so regularly and so mysteriously, the family who own the knife would undoubtedly have second thoughts about donating it to us.'

Slightly could see this might be a bit awkward, but it didn't seem to her nearly as interesting as the thefts themselves. She tried to get Mr John back on track.

'What about clues?' she asked eagerly. 'Did you

find a cigar stub dropped at the scene of the crime? Or a scrap of curiously dyed cloth caught on a nail? Or a tendency of the thief to steal only items beginning with the letter K?'

Mr John looked at her in some surprise.

'Not really,' he said. 'In fact, the thefts appear to have followed no pattern at all.'

'What do you mean?'

'Well, my dear, let me see if I can explain.' He paused for a moment, as if trying to think how best to speak to a stupid person. Slightly gritted her teeth to keep from snipping at him.

'It's like this,' he said. 'It is normal to expect jewel thieves to steal jewels. And art thieves to steal paintings. But this seems to be a totally random thief. Each item taken has no discernible connection to the next. Which means we can't figure out what sort of thief we're looking for, or where he is likely to strike next. I have with me a list . . .'

With a careful deliberation that made Slightly want to poke him with her fork, Mr John brought out a sheet of paper from his breast pocket, unfolded it and smoothed it out on the table. But when he showed them the catalogue of stolen items, she forgot her irritation. He was right. It *was* a most perplexing list. It included an oil sketch by Rembrandt, a piece of blue stalactite from France, some musical instruments, a set of seventeenth-century silver spoons, a gilt statue of Buddha, some pewter mugs with hinged lids, a stuffed marmot, some Flemish tapestries, a gold brooch decorated with a jade rabbit . . .

Mr John stared glumly at the list. 'We also expect thieves to try to *sell* what they've stolen, and to that end we have invested a great deal of effort and money in having the black market watched. Also the ports – Dover, Newcastle and, of course, Greenock – in case the artefacts are being smuggled out of the country. But with no results. It's as if the objects stolen from the Museum have vanished into thin air.'

'Fascinating!' breathed Slightly. 'And you're telling us that there isn't even one single, solitary clue?'

'Well, yes, there is *one* thing. We have photos of what looks like the paw print of an animal – possibly an ape? – and some round marks that a number of my fellow trustees believe were made by the tip of a wooden leg, though this seems fanciful to me.'

'These marks – were they in blood?' asked Slightly, feeling that at last they were getting somewhere.

Mr John looked shocked that a little girl would have such a thought. 'Certainly not!' he exclaimed. 'They were in ink. The ink that is made available so that people may sign the Visitors' Book. The inkwell was stolen – nothing is safe from these reprobates! – but the thief accidentally spilt some of the ink onto the floor in the process. And –'

'– and then stepped in it!' cried Slightly. *The best kind of clue,* she crowed to herself, *is the serendipitous kind!* 'I would love to see those prints!'

Mr John smiled condescendingly. 'The photos taken of them are in a drawer in my desk. I'm not at all sure they would be appropriate viewing for young ladies.' Slightly was finding it hard not to lose her temper. Mr Sherlock Holmes didn't get treated like this! She also felt thoroughly stumped. Glasgow was hundreds of miles away, and *any* detective would have trouble solving a case at such long distance.

But then Mr Malcolm spoke up.

'John, you know I have decided to return north with you for a visit – it's been far too long since I was home. But here's a thought. How would it be if we invite Granny and Slightly to accompany us? There are many fine things to see in Glasgow and a change of scene might be just the thing to banish the nightmares that Granny tells me have been troubling you, Slightly.' He smiled at her. 'Nobody has bad dreams in Glasgow!'

'Except Mr John,' said Slightly without thinking – then clamped both hands over her mouth.

Too late!

'How on earth did you know my brother was having bad dreams?' asked Mr Malcolm, and, at the same time, Mr John bellowed, 'SHE WASN'T A DREAM!'

There was a horrible pause. Slightly felt all eyes upon her and gulped. She was in trouble now for sure.

'Slightly Jones!' said Granny in a deeply disapproving voice. 'Have you been *eavesdropping*?!'

Then something surprising happened.

'Please don't be angry with the little girl,' said Mr John. 'I was very likely speaking too loudly last night. And you know, I think I should thank her! It may be that I *need* to bring this out into the open. I have been deeply troubled. Though if word of what I am about to say should reach the ears of my business associates, they would certainly think I'd gone mad, and I would be ruined.'

'We are honourable people here, Mr John,' said Granny, though she gave Slightly a hard look as she said it. 'You may speak in perfect confidence.'

Mr John gave her a solemn nod, and paused as if to gather his thoughts.

'Some years ago I loved a lady. Her name was Miss Jenny McGuire. She was as lovely as a flower and, sadly, as fragile. That year the summer was unusually hot, and diseases of every sort bred in the putrid air of Glasgow. I begged her to leave, to go out into the country to safeguard her health. She agreed, but it was already too late.'

There was a sympathetic sigh from each person in the room.

'She was buried in the Necropolis, a cemetery on a green hill by the cathedral, overlooking the city, yet away from the noise and grime. A peaceful place. Or so I believed.'

'What happened to change this belief?' asked Granny.

'What happened was . . . I saw her.'

There was a general stir, but no one spoke.

'It started just as the trouble at the Museum began,' Mr John continued. 'She came to me in the night, a white shape at the foot of my bed, lit by some strange, other-worldly light. And she was trying to tell me something.'

'What was it?' Slightly whispered.

Mr John shook his head. 'At first I couldn't say. Her voice was always soft . . . Night after night she came and I struggled to hear her, and night after night I failed. I began to wonder, was she trying to tell me who the thief was? Perhaps she had sensed how troubled I was and had come back from the grave to help me?'

Slightly's eyes went wide. *A ghost detective!* she thought, but she managed to stay quiet.

'It seems, however, that her message for me was more personal than that. The night finally came when her words *did* break through, and once more I heard her sweet voice. She spoke in Gaelic, just as we had always done. She said, "Tha do thoileachas anns an uaigh", which means "Your happiness is in the grave".'

'Oh, John,' said Mr Malcolm mournfully.

'Yes,' said Mr John. 'She was telling me that all hope of happiness had died with her. Was buried with her. She was telling me that the restlessness I have felt all these years must be subdued. I must throw myself into my work even more than before. That is the way to find contentment. As soon as I understood this, my visions stopped. Now my nights are undisturbed, except for my worries for the Museum.' He drew a deep breath, and managed a weak smile. 'There has been no one I dared mention a word of this to,' he said. 'Speaking of it has eased my mind more than you can imagine.' Then he turned to Granny. 'And now may I add my own invitation to my brother's. Please, will you and Miss Slightly come to Glasgow?'

Even though she knew this wasn't a good time to draw attention to herself, Slightly couldn't help leaping onto her feet with excitement. But Granny put out a restraining hand.

'It is a most kind invitation,' she said to Mr John. 'We'll see, shall we?'

Slightly gave Granny her best big-eyed, pleading look.

'I said, 'We'll see,' repeated Granny firmly.

And with that, Slightly had to be content.

Chapter Four:

On to the Second City in the Empire

Mr John might not have been angry about being 'overheard' but Granny certainly was. Slightly was in disgrace, to the point where she feared Granny might actually refuse to consider the Glasgow invitation!

But Slightly really, *really* wanted to go. So, in the days that followed, she was on her best behaviour . . . and gradually Granny's *we'll see* turned into a *thank you, we will.*

Slightly was deliriously happy and, in a calmer way, so was Mr John because the wealthy family had agreed to donate the sacrificial knife to the Hunterian Museum. It was a wonderful acquisition. With his business in London complete, there was nothing else to keep them. They would be leaving from the brick and wrought-iron splendour of Euston Station, heading north, mile after mile, the length of England, on into Scotland – further from home than Slightly had ever gone before . . .

'I can't wait!' she cried on the morning of their departure.

'Hold *still*!' said Granny, struggling to get the brush through Slightly's hair. 'This mop gets tidied or we're going *nowhere*!' And with every stroke, Granny gave Slightly a piece of her mind. 'Now, remember, I'm expecting you to *behave* yourself. There is to be no losing your temper. No eavesdropping or snooping or prying. Don't go poking your nose into things that don't concern you!'

You might as well say, don't be a detective! thought Slightly rebelliously, but all she said out loud was, 'OW!'

More advice followed until, as the last red tangle of hair was subdued, Granny gave her final warning.

'Remember, I'll be watching you, Slightly Jones!'

'Cab's here!' Mr Malcolm called up from downstairs.

Finally! And Slightly escaped with a whoop and a grin.

The trip through the busy streets seemed to take forever, but at last they climbed down from their hansom cab and hurried into the bustle of noise, steam and soot that was Euston Station.

'There he is!' cried Slightly. 'There's Mr John!'

He was waiting for them by the train, and as Slightly ran towards him she noticed a leather valise held tightly in his arms.

'Is that it? Is that Captain Cook's sacrificial knife all the way from the South Pacific?' she called out, but Mr John scowled and put a finger to his lips, looking around to see if anyone had heard her words.

Slightly started to scowl right back, then, with a rueful rub of her head, she remembered Granny's advice. Besides, she couldn't be *really* angry – not on the brink of her very first train ride!

Mr John urged them all into the carriage. Whistles blew, steam shrilled, the great wheels lurched and slipped and got a grip on the rails so that slowly, slowly, and then picking up speed, the locomotive and all its tail of coaches headed out of the station, into the morning and on towards the north.

'What's that building?' exclaimed Slightly, bouncing on and off her seat and pressing her nose to the window. 'Look at that! Are we out of London already? What kind of factory is that? Look – a cow!'

However, the trip was going to take all day, and the adults (Mr John in particular) were relieved to discover that not even Slightly could keep up such a high level of excitement for *that* long. Gradually the number of questions dwindled and she made herself comfortable on the upholstered seats with her feet on the warmers Mr John had hired against the chill. She read the Penny Dreadful Mr Malcolm had bought her when Granny wasn't looking. Granny did *not* approve of Penny Dreadfuls, but Slightly read them every chance she got. She loved having her spine tingled by tales of mad murderers, adventures among the cannibals, hair-raising highwaymen and the Living Dead. She stared at the highly dramatic picture of the Mysterious Stranger, his curved dagger held high over the terrified maiden, black candles and mystical symbols marked on the walls (*probably using his own blood – or perhaps the blood of earlier victims,* thought Slightly with a delicious shiver). There was also an instalment of a story titled 'The Headless Skeleton and the Undead' which spent far too long with nothing happening and then cut off just as the corpses started to reach for the hero – very frustrating! When she'd finished Slightly lent it to

Mr Malcolm, who read it cover to cover. Then Mr John did the same, though he kept stopping to say, 'Really, Malcolm, what could *possibly* have made you think this was appropriate reading material for our young guest?'

Slightly felt herself getting cross again, but Mr Malcolm just winked at her and paid no attention to his brother's fussing.

Perhaps there is something about a long train journey that encourages reminiscing. Particularly so in the privacy of a First Class carriage. As the train thundered through the changing landscape (green fields and woods, market towns and sooty cities) and Granny snoozed in the corner, the Gentler brothers talked and laughed and told stories about their boyhood and Slightly listened.

She'd never had a brother or sister. It didn't bother her. But now, looking at Mr Malcolm and Mr John, Slightly couldn't help wondering what it would feel like to be them. It was strange to think how many experiences they had shared as children, growing up in the same house, allied against the same rules and restrictions, planning midnight raids together to Mrs Mull's kitchen, facing the discipline of their ferociously strict father side by side.

'Though John always got the fewest swipes of

Father's cane and the most apple tarts to help him get over them,' Mr Malcolm said with a rueful smile. 'Mrs Mull always loved you best, little brother,' he added. 'But then she'd feel bad, and sneak me some extra to make up for it!'

'Can I ask you something?' said Slightly.

'What, about how to get round Mrs Mull?' said Mr John. 'Don't worry – she'll be so pleased to have a young person in the house again, you'll be able to have as many tarts as you want!'

'It wasn't that – though that's good to know. No, I was wondering why you call Mr John your *little* brother, Mr Malcolm? He's taller than you, and he must be older, to have inherited the business and all . . . ?' She had a pretty shrewd feeling she was being impertinent, asking questions like this, but she was too curious to stop. Besides, Granny couldn't hear her when she was asleep!

'I call him little brother because he *is* my little brother,' said Mr Malcolm. 'I'm the elder.'

'Oh!' said Slightly, confused and beginning to get embarrassed. 'I didn't mean . . .'

'No, no. We don't mind you asking, do we, John?' said Mr Malcolm with a smile, though Slightly couldn't help thinking that Mr John didn't look quite so at ease with her prying. She was glad all over again that Mr Malcolm was the brother who lived with her at Limpopo House!

'I was always more interested in music than in business,' Mr Malcolm continued, 'but our father never understood why I would choose *anything* over the life he'd planned for me. I think he thought he could beat my dreams out of me.' He looked so sad, for a moment Slightly wanted to hug him, but then he shrugged and gave her a wry grin. 'But then I got too old to beat and old enough to leave! I came to London, and then to Limpopo House, and there I lived happily ever after.'

There was a pause, and then Mr John burst out, 'As soon as I had money of my own, I offered to share with you!'

'And by then, I had no need of it.' Mr Malcolm patted his brother's knee. 'Don't worry, I'm sure Slightly isn't thinking that you're like those bad usurping brothers in the Penny Dreadful stories!'

'Er, oh no, of course not!' said Slightly, although that was exactly what she *had* been thinking.

She was finding she couldn't seem to keep one steady opinion of Mr John for any length of time. He was such a mixture of things. Smug and kind. Rude and polite. Condescending and irritating and fond of his brother. As a trainee detective she ought to be able to work him out but she just couldn't. It was quite tiring! Very tiring, in fact . . . Very . . .

When Slightly woke from her nap the short autumn afternoon was over. They were moving through the outskirts of a city, past darkened factories and dimly lit tenements.

'Are we there yet?' she asked, yawning.

'Very nearly,' said Mr John. Even as he spoke, they could feel the train begin to slow down.

A sudden shriek from the wheels woke Granny with a snort and an urgent cry of, 'Ahoy! Fishcakes!' which made everyone laugh – a good way to end any journey. The train pulled into the station with a final puff of smoke and steam.

'And here we are!' said Mr John, helping Granny onto the platform. (Slightly jumped down before he could do the same for her since she was quite big enough to get out of a train by herself, thank you very much!) 'Welcome to Glasgow – the Second City of the Empire!'

In the cab, Mr John did all the talking, extolling the virtues of his city non-stop. Clearly he was delighted to be home, but Slightly found his relentless enthusiasm a bit hard to take. Industry, inventions, literature, art . . . there didn't seem to be anything *his* city hadn't done first, and better.

Even traffic jams!

'We won't be going along the street the Hunterian is on,' he explained, 'because they're digging the tunnel for our new Underground train system up in that area. The traffic gets quite slow at this time of day.'

'We already have an Underground in London,' Slightly couldn't resist saying.

'Yes, and isn't it a horribly smoky affair?'

'Well . . .' In the enclosed space of the tunnels, the lurching steam trains blasted soot and smoke all over the passengers. It *was* pretty awful.

'That's what I thought,' said Mr John smugly. 'But here in Glasgow, we've solved that problem!' He explained to her how, instead of each train having an engine, there would be one huge *stationary* engine and the trains were to be pulled around the great circle of tunnels by an incredibly strong cable.

'No smoke, no soot, just reliable transportation!'

Slightly wanted to argue but in fact it sounded like a really good idea. Before she could bring herself to say so, though, Mr John grabbed her arm.

'Look! There it is, up on the hill,' he cried, pointing. 'Glasgow University, home of Glasgow's finest museum!'

Slightly craned her neck to see. It was certainly a

fine sight, perched on a tree-covered hill and looking like a castle and a cathedral rolled into one.

At last – the Hunterian! The scene of the crimes! Slightly opened her mouth to start interrogating Mr John, but Granny gave a meaningful cough and a firm shake of the head.

Slightly subsided, fuming inside. Frustratingly, Mr John chose this point to go quiet too, so she was getting *no* chance to pick up clues.

Oh well, she thought, *at least he's stopped boasting.* They'd reached the West End of the city now and she was free to stare out of the window at all the grand and imposing houses. Slightly wondered what sort of people lived in them? And then, as the carriage turned in at a fine gravelled driveway, she realised that, for a while anyway, it would be people like her!

As they pulled up at the grand front door, Slightly's mouth fell open. The Gentler mansion would have swallowed a good number of Limpopo Houses without difficulty. It was huge! Built out of reddish stone, it was the most *solid* building Slightly had ever seen. Empires might rise and fall, but this house was going nowhere!

'You live *here*?' she asked Mr John, impressed in spite of herself.

'Oh, yes. Ugly great pile, isn't it? When our

grandfather built it, he wanted to make something that said *Look at me – I'm here. I've arrived.* And now, so have we!' He pulled open the door of the cab and jumped down. 'Come in! Come in! I telegraphed Mrs Mull that I was bringing guests . . .'

Slightly hung back. She was feeling out of place. Granny too was silent, and Mr Malcolm tapped a nervous rhythm on his trouser leg with his fingers.

They all trailed up the wide steps, through the grand front doors and on into an even grander entrance hall. The fine marble floor stretched away to a double staircase sweeping impressively upwards. On either side of the hall, half-open doors gave Slightly glimpses of elegant reception rooms crowded with carved fireplaces and heavy furniture covered with dust sheets. The chandeliers were bagged and the hearths empty. It was as if the owner had gone away and forgotten to return.

It made Slightly sad.

Just then Granny began to sneeze.

'I . . . ACHOO . . . beg your . . . ACHOO . . . pardon!' she said, rummaging in her pocket for a handkerchief. 'ACHOOOO!'

The sound echoed.

'You haven't changed a thing,' said Mr Malcolm in a strange, strained voice.

'No. It's just as it was when Father died,' said Mr John. Then he put a hand on his brother's arm. 'What's wrong, Malcolm?'

Slightly could see that her friend did, indeed, seem unwell. He didn't answer.

Mr John looked around. 'You're right, of course. It *is* gloomy. I don't notice, normally. There's little point in unwrapping rooms I don't ever use.'

Slightly couldn't imagine this as a place full of life, but then Mr John remembered his duties as host.

'Come, it's not *all* like a mausoleum!' he cried. 'My own rooms are quite snug and Mrs Mull will be delighted to have some company to look after. I'm afraid I live too much the life of a dull dog for her taste! Oh, and speaking of dogs . . .'

There was a frantic clatter of paws trying to get purchase on the polished floors and then, tail and ears flying, the most unlikely looking hound Slightly had ever seen came bursting round the corner. His joy at seeing Mr John was in direct conflict with his equally powerful desire to greet every one of the newcomers, which made for a wild few moments of woofling, sliding sideways into people and swinging his tail so hard into the walls that Slightly feared he would hurt himself.

She saw Mr Malcolm wading through the chaos to

hug a round, grey-haired woman who had appeared, calling the dog to order with absolutely no effect. *That must be Mrs Mull,* she deduced, and she was right.

'Enough, Mack!' The housekeeper's voice finally found a pitch to reach the canine brain and, after one more mad race round Mr John, the dog collapsed happily across his master's feet, stopped barking and grinned at everyone.

'That's better,' said Mrs Mull with a curtsey and a smile. 'Please be welcomed to Gentler House, Miss Tonic, Miss Jones. And forgive my boys – all three of them!'

Chapter Five:

Night-time Prowlers and Daytime Ducks

Mrs Mull had aired two fine, large, old-fashioned bedrooms for Mr John's female guests. Fires were banked up in the fireplaces, lighting everything with a soft glow.

'I'm going to sleep like a log!' yawned Slightly widely, forgetting to cover her mouth. (Granny must have been pretty tired too, because she didn't make her usual comment about being able to see all the way to China.) Before Granny had quite closed the door on her, Slightly's head hit the pillow and she plunged deep, deep into sleep . . .

. . . until the crying started. It was an achingly unhappy sound. Someone was very sad, and she wanted to comfort them, but where were they? She couldn't see anyone. And where was *she*? This wasn't home – she didn't know where it was – if only the crying would stop! If only . . .

Slightly sat up with a gasp. Her heart was pounding and her hands were sweaty, but as she looked about in the dim light, gradually she was able to calm down.

She wasn't lost at all. She was in Glasgow, in the Gentler mansion, in bed, in the middle of the night.

'It was just another nightmare,' she murmured. 'Just a . . .' The words froze in her throat as she realised that even though the dream was over, the crying wasn't! She was wide awake, yet she could still hear the same sad whimpering. And it was right outside her door. Something horribly unhappy was desperate to get into her room.

Slightly tried to call out, but her voice was hiding in her throat. She tried again.

'Who . . . who's there?'

To her huge relief, the answer was a bark.

'Mack? Mack, is that you?!' she cried, scrambling out of bed and rushing to the door. She expected the big dog to come bounding in as soon as she opened the door, but he didn't. Instead he stayed out in the dark corridor and whined at her. He was obviously trying to tell her something important in Dog!

'I'll just go with you then, shall I?' Slightly said.

That seemed to be the right response. As soon as she lit her candle and came out into the corridor, Mack woofled urgently and padded off. Shivering a little, Slightly followed.

There were cold draughts blowing over her bare feet. Her candle made a tiny pool of light, but all around her she was aware of the great, dark, silent, empty house. *All those rooms,* she thought, *all those unlived-in rooms, shuttered up, with nobody in them, not for years and years.*

'Where are we going, Mack?' she whispered, but it seemed they were already there.

The door to one of the rooms was open. Mack led Slightly inside.

By the dim light of her candle, she could see the ghostly, sheet-covered shapes of furniture. The pictures on the walls were time-stained portraits of Gentler ancestors in dark clothes – only the faces showed pale and indistinct. When one of them moved, Slightly almost swallowed her tongue, until she realised she was looking into a dusty mirror and the face was her own.

She gave herself an impatient shake and was just

turning to go back to bed when . . .

. . . in the room, between her and the door, someone sighed.

Slowly, terrified, Slightly held up her shaking candle.

There, in a dark dressing gown and slippers, so that only his face showed white, stood Mr Malcolm. He was staring right at her, his eyes wide open. They were glassy and blank and strange, as if he were seeing something that wasn't there. Or perhaps something inside his head. He sighed again, a deep, unhappy breath.

Mack whined and pressed against Slightly's legs. She tried to speak, but then Mr Malcolm abruptly turned around and walked away.

'I think he must be sleepwalking, the way he used to,' Slightly told Mack. She was sure she'd read somewhere that you must never wake a sleepwalker, though she wasn't quite sure why. 'We'd better follow him.'

And so they did, a strange midnight procession through the empty mansion. Finally, though, Mr Malcolm seemed to feel he'd had enough exercise. Still without speaking, he led the way to his own room and had just gone inside when Mr John stuck his head out of *his* room and yelped in surprise.

'Miss Slightly! You startled me!' he exclaimed. 'I thought I heard a noise and . . . what are *you* doing here?!'

'Mack woke me up,' Slightly explained. 'He led me to Mr Malcolm. I think he was sleepwalking!' She looked at the closed door. 'Though he seems to have stopped now,' she added uncertainly.

Mr John came out and turned up the gas in the corridor. He sighed. 'Oh dear,' he said. 'Perhaps it wasn't a good idea for him to come back here. He used to sleepwalk as a boy, especially when my father had been particularly harsh with him.'

'He never sleepwalks at home – I mean, at Limpopo House,' said Slightly.

'It's the memories,' said Mr John, shaking his head sadly. 'My father was a hard man. After our mother died, Malcolm was never happy here.'

Slightly shivered. 'Will he be all right?' she asked anxiously.

'Oh, yes. He'll sleep till morning now. And he'll remember nothing of this.' Mr John looked earnestly at her and lowered his voice. 'I think the kindest thing would be to leave it that way, don't you? He would be most upset to think he'd frightened you.'

Slightly had to smile. 'I pretty much frightened myself,' she said. 'But I promise I won't say a word.'

So it was agreed. Mack settled down outside Mr Malcolm's door, while Mr John escorted Slightly back to her room.

It was a long time before she finally fell asleep again.

The rest of the night passed uneventfully and Slightly woke the next morning feeling surprisingly rested. But when she bounced into Granny's room, she discovered to her dismay that Granny had had a terrible night. Her sneezing fit the evening before had marked the beginning of a heavy cold.

'I thought it was just dust. How stupid,' Granny snuffled. 'I *can't* be having a cold in someone else's house!' (Though what she actually said was, 'I *cand* be hafink a co'd in sudone else's 'ouse!')

Slightly patted her arm sympathetically and ran off to find Mrs Mull in the kitchen, where she explained the situation. She looked about for Mr John and Mr Malcolm there as well, but Mrs Mull directed her to the formal dining room. There was a definite suggestion of shock in her voice that Slightly should have thought anything else.

'You go along and have some breakfast now, Miss, and I'll go up to your grandmother this instant.'

Slightly was about to explain that Granny wasn't really her grandmother, but Mrs Mull had already gone, skirts rustling. She had a look in her eyes that was full of purpose.

Uh oh, Slightly thought with a not entirely nice grin. *I think Granny's about to be nursed to within an inch of her life!*

When she managed to *find* the dining room, the Gentler brothers confirmed her suspicions.

'I am sorry Granny is unwell,' said Mr Malcolm. He was looking a little dark-eyed, but otherwise untroubled by his night-time prowling. 'Still, I know Mrs Mull will have a wonderful time looking after her!'

'When she's not feeling mortified that Glasgow made our guest ill, that is,' added Mr John.

'Really, Slightly, don't worry. There's nothing Mrs Mull loves more than an invalid. It's the nicest thing Granny could possibly have done for her,' Mr Malcolm reassured her. 'And the best thing *we* can do is leave her to get on with it. So, little brother, will we be taking the knife to the Museum this morning?'

'And observing the scene of the crimes?' added Slightly. She was keen to start detecting.

The evening before, Mr John had told them

the knife was now locked up in a safe in his study. 'I use it for important business documents and contracts. And I keep the key on a silver chain – see? – which I wear round my neck at all times. Not even that friend of yours, Master Bone the pickpocket, could get this!' he'd said smugly to Slightly.

Slightly, on the other hand, was pretty sure that if he put his mind to it, Matthew could steal the false teeth out of the mouth of the King of Belgium. (It wouldn't be very polite to say that to her host, though, so she hadn't.)

But now it was the morning of a new day and she looked at Mr John eagerly, her head buzzing with thoughts of clues and crime. She couldn't understand how he could be acting so calm! *He's eating his breakfast as if it were the only thing in the world! Still, we'll be on our way soon . . .*

So she was thoroughly shocked to hear him say, setting down his teacup, 'Oh, I have no plans to go to the Museum today. I have to attend to the business – I've been away too long!' He folded his napkin and stood up. 'Besides, it's my opinion the knife is safer here than in the Museum.' He patted his coat where the key was hidden, and gave Slightly a look as if to say, '*Don't worry, little girl, everything's under control!*'

'But –' Slightly started to protest, but Mr John was already on his way out of the door.

'Malcolm, you'll entertain our young visitor, I'm sure,' he called over his shoulder.

Slightly turned to Mr Malcolm indignantly. '*Young visitor?!*' she exclaimed through gritted teeth. 'Why does he treat me like a child?'

Mr Malcolm smiled into his teacup but said nothing.

Slightly threw herself down on a chair and sighed.

'Because I *am* a child,' she answered herself. She had a face as long as a wet washday. 'What was the point of coming all this way? If your brother keeps all the clues from me, how can I possibly do my job, solve the mystery and find the thief?'

'You can't,' said Mr Malcolm firmly. 'So after we've each had a large, sustaining breakfast, I suggest we do something about it.' He wouldn't say another word until he had served her, and himself, brimming platefuls of eggs, sausages, kidneys, bacon . . .

Since she was, in fact, really hungry, Slightly gave in. Even Mr Sherlock Holmes was known to have enjoyed a good breakfast and, obviously, fainting from hunger was a handicap to detecting. But the moment she was full and Mr Gentler had finished his last cup of tea, she jumped up.

'Well?'

Mr John stood up too. 'Now, before Mrs Mull comes in to tidy or Granny calls for you to brush your hair or polish your boots, I suggest we go for a walk – and I know just the place . . .'

Victoria Park was not far – just a brisk stroll away. It felt good to be away from the sad memories of the Gentler mansion. In spite of a chilly breeze, the day was fine, and the water of the lake reflected a clear blue sky. This far from the city centre, the soot and smoke and dirty air could be forgotten for a while. They settled themselves on a bench by the water's edge.

'Right,' said Mr Malcolm. 'To business! Miss Jones, if you would be so kind as to take the minutes, I will call this meeting to order.' He bowed and Slightly did her best to bob a curtsey back – not an easy thing to do while sitting.

'First, perhaps you would like to make a copy of the list of stolen items. I just happened to be, ah, passing my brother's desk this morning and accidentally picked it and this envelope of photographs up . . .' said Mr Malcolm.

'Mr Malcolm!' gasped Slightly in delight. 'I believe you have the makings of a criminal!'

Mr Malcolm grinned. 'To be honest, I'd be happy to get them back before John discovers I borrowed them! So I will read, you will write, and we shall both think hard.'

It was a strange, random list, as Mr John had said, made up of a collection of apparently unrelated objects from every department of the Museum – paintings, textiles, silver, jewellery, statues, animal and mineral specimens.

'It really does make no sense,' said Mr Malcolm when he had read them all out. 'What reason could any thief in his right mind have for stealing these particular objects? Why would someone who wanted to nick a silver seventeenth-century spoon set also want to take a painting of the seaside? Why would the same someone then come back and steal a small gilt statue of Buddha and a stuffed marmot?'

For a long moment, Slightly stared at the list of things in her notebook and sucked on the end of her silver pencil.

Then she noticed something.

'You know, there's nothing on this list that's *big*,' she said. 'No stuffed polar bears or elephants, for example.'

Mr Malcolm looked at her thoughtfully. 'That's true. It's all either quite small, or else, like the tapestries, can be rolled up quite small. What do you think that means?'

'I've no idea. I'll make a note of it, though.' And under the list of missing objects, she wrote: *All small. No polar bears. Meaning?*

'Let's see the photos next,' she said. 'Maybe they'll give us a clue.'

So Mr Malcolm brought out the photos of the strange inky paw print and the mark like a peg leg and laid them on the bench between them. Even in the bright sunshine, they made Slightly shiver a little.

'How do you suppose he lost his leg?' she said, looking up with big eyes. 'Maybe it was bitten off by an enormous white whale. Or a shark.'

'Or maybe a crocodile,' suggested Mr Malcolm. 'In the depths of a jungle, somewhere exotic and hot and far away.'

'Where he captured a chimpanzee – or a small orang-utan! – and tamed it . . .'

'. . . and trained it to break and enter, and steal random things from museums,' concluded Mr Malcolm. Slightly giggled . . . and then suddenly grabbed him by the arm so hard he squawked.

'Somewhere exotic and hot and far away,' she said urgently. 'Take that idea a bit further and what do you have?'

'Mosquito bites?' said Mr Malcolm, rubbing his arm. 'Painful sunburn?'

'No!' cried Slightly. '*Occult pagan rituals!*'

She said this in a louder voice than she should have, causing a nursery maid pushing her young charge in a pram to gasp and scuttle away quickly.

'Occult pagan rituals?' repeated Mr Gentler in a lower voice. 'That's more than *a bit* further! Where did you even *hear* of such things?'

'The Penny Dreadfuls, of course! You can learn a lot from them.'

'Ah,' said Mr Malcolm. 'Best not let Granny hear you say that.'

'No, but think about it!' whispered Slightly excitedly. 'What if this thief is more than just a thief – what if he's *an evil, demon-worshipping, criminal mastermind*? What if while he was off in some far-away place, taming orang-utans . . .'

'. . . and getting his leg bitten off by crocodiles.'

'Yes – what if he was *also* initiated into a strange, demonic, occult, pagan religion where they do these strange, demonic, occult, pagan rituals? And what if he's stealing these seemingly random things from the Museum so he can perform those very same rituals *right here in Britain*?' Slightly had turned quite pink with excitement.

'Well . . .' said Mr Malcolm. 'It's a little hard to imagine a demonic ritual that makes use of –' and he consulted the list – 'a porcelain teapot, a small guitar, and an inlaid tortoiseshell hairbrush.'

Slightly shrugged her shoulders dismissively. What Mr Malcolm said was true, but she was not about to let go of her evil, devil-worshipping, criminal mastermind idea.

'I think you're forgetting what Mr Sherlock Holmes said . . . well, I can't remember either, but it was something like "When you have eliminated things, whatever you haven't, um, eliminated is probably *the* thing, er, unless it's impossible". Something like that, anyway. Of course he said it better.'

'Well, I'm sure that's very true,' said Mr Malcolm, though he looked a bit confused. 'And of course we haven't even been to the Museum yet.'

Slightly kicked impatiently at a pebble on the path.

'Mr Sherlock Holmes wouldn't need to go to the Museum. He'd be able to solve the case just by looking at the evidence. We need to look *harder*.'

And they did look harder, turning the photographs this way and that and rereading the list of stolen artefacts, but still they came up with nothing.

'Let's take a break before our brains start to smoke,' said Mr Malcolm eventually. 'I brought some bread – we can feed the ducks.'

'What ducks?' said Slightly, grumpy and discouraged. 'I don't see any ducks.'

'Oh, don't worry, they'll come,' Mr Malcolm told her. 'They're always on the lookout.' And he was right. As soon as they started throwing bits of bread into the water, ducks appeared from all directions, rushing for the food with white wakes and squabbling beaks.

'See? Throw the bread and, as if by magic, the ducks arrive,' said Mr Malcolm.

Slightly said nothing. If Mr Malcolm had looked at her he would have seen a very peculiar expression on her face. But Mr Malcolm didn't look.

'This case is a real puzzler,' he continued. 'If only we could stop being one step *behind* all the time, and start being one step *ahead*.'

Still Slightly was silent. A piece of bread lay, unthrown, in the palm of her hand.

'The ducks are too shy to come right to you,' said Mr Malcolm, noticing the bread. 'I've tried many times and never suc– OWW!'

Without warning, Slightly had grabbed his arm again.

'My dear, I wish you'd stop doing that,' protested

Mr Malcolm. 'I assure you, I *am* paying attention to what you're saying, though you weren't actually saying anything just then.'

'But are you paying attention to what *you're* saying?' Slightly squeaked excitedly.

'About what – about ducks?' said Mr Malcolm with a puzzled frown.

'No! Well, yes. *You* said that if we throw the bread the ducks will come. And *then* you said, what we need is to be ahead of the game for a change. Don't you see? What we need is to know what's going to be stolen next. What we need is bread . . . for burglars!'

'Bait!' cried Mr Malcolm, slapping his forehead with his hand.

'Exactly,' said Slightly. She jumped up and did a dance on the spot, panicking ducks right, left and centre. 'Bait! Something no bigger than the other items on the list, something new to the Museum, something valuable and maybe, just maybe, something attractive to a demon-worshipper! Something like *an ancient sacrificial knife brought back by Captain Cook from the strange, exotic South Pacific*!'

For a moment, the two could only stare at each other in delight.

'We are *cunning*!' Mr Malcolm announced to the world at large. Then he frowned. 'But will we be able to convince John to risk it? I seriously doubt it. He's reluctant to take the knife out of the safe at home, remember, let alone try to catch a thief with it.'

'We'll have to *make* him.' And Slightly stamped her foot. 'There's another problem, though,' she added. 'Mr John's been so careful not to let anyone know what was in the wind – not even Matthew Bone! But there's no good putting out bait if the thief isn't even aware that the knife exists. The ducks showed up for the bread because they were already on the lookout.'

'So how do we get the news to our thief that we've got some extra-special bread waiting just for him?' murmured Mr Malcolm.

Slightly stared at him, admiration all over her face.

'Mr Malcolm, you've done it again,' she cried. 'You're a *genius*!'

'I am?'

'You most certainly are. You said *the news*. And where do you find *the news* . . . ?'

She watched delightedly as understanding dawned.

'IN A NEWSPAPER!' chorused Mr Malcolm and Slightly Jones.

Chapter Six:

Mr John's Cunning Plan

'This is outrageous!' cried Mr John, striding furiously into the dining room the next morning.

Slightly choked guiltily on her toast. *Oh no, he's found out it was us!* she thought in a panic.

But Mr Malcolm went on calmly eating.

'What's the matter, little brother?' he said.

'What's the matter? *This* is the matter!' And Mr John waved a sheaf of newspapers at them. 'I can't for the life of me *imagine* where they get their information!'

'What information is that?' Mr Malcolm asked innocently.

'Captain Cook's knife!' Mr John bellowed, flinging the newspapers down on the table with fine disregard for teacups and fried eggs. 'The devils . . . er,' (here he glanced at Slightly) 'I mean, the naughty men have found out about Captain Cook's knife!'

The headlines blared out at them:

'Rare Knife Brought back from Pacific Voyage of Captain Cook Acquired for Hunterian'

'Exhibit Opens Today!'

'Another Triumph for Our Great Glasgow Museum'

'There was stiff competition from other museums, says trustee John Gentler, but the Hunterian's fine reputation won the day!'

Slightly could feel a nervous giggle trying to escape from her throat. Their daring leak to the newspapers had been a success! The reporter Mr Malcolm had contacted didn't suspect for a moment that he was being given lies. And Granny hadn't been around to wonder what she and Mr Malcolm had been getting up to!

Mr John was pacing up and down the dining room, fuming.

'I never said *one word* to the papers!' he growled. 'There's even some piffle about pagan rituals.'

'Oh!' exclaimed Slightly. 'They put that in?'

Mr Malcolm kicked her under the table. 'I mean, they put that *sort of thing* in . . . ?'

'See for yourself,' Mr John grunted. 'On the next page.'

Slightly turned the page, and there, beside another article titled: 'More Ghostly Sightings in Graveyard' were the words: 'Connection with Pagan Sacrificial Rituals Firmly Denied By Museum Trustee and Well Known Shipping Magnate John Gentler'

She sniggered silently to herself but managed to keep a straight face.

'Well, the cat's out of the bag now, little brother,' said Mr Malcolm. 'You'll have to get the knife to the Museum right away. Still, look on the bright side. It'll certainly bring in the crowds!'

He turned to Slightly.

She took her cue.

'Oh, but bless us, Mr John, what if it brings in the thief as well?' she said, clasping her hands and looking theatrically concerned.

But Mr John didn't notice her overacting. He was too busy falling into the next stage of their cunning trap. 'What's that? The thief . . .' he said with a thoughtful frown. 'You could just be right there. This might very well be the thief's next target. How could he resist such a wonderful artefact?

He couldn't, no matter who he is. It would be irresistible. Irresistible *bait* . . .'

'Bait? Oh, but wouldn't that be *much* too risky?' Slightly piped up. Mr Malcolm gave her a warning look, but she didn't care. She was enjoying herself!

'Not necessarily, my dear young lady,' said Mr John, sounding more than a little smug. 'We could focus our attention on guarding the Captain Cook knife. Up until now, you see,' he explained patiently, 'we've always been one step behind this thief. This unfortunate newspaper leak could be just what we need to put us one step *ahead*!'

'Oh, Mr *John*!' cooed Slightly.' How *clever*!' *Steady on,* she warned herself, *or he'll smell a rat!*

But Mr John smelt nothing. Not even breakfast. He was already heading out of the door, eager to put the cunning plan – *his* cunning plan – into action.

Granny was on the mend, but she was still not well enough to go out to the Museum with the others.

'Now, Slightly,' she croaked. 'I'm counting on you to *behave* yourself. Any time you think you might be about to lose your temper or start poking your nose into other people's business, I want you to stop. I want you to say to yourself – even though I'm not actually there – *Granny is watching me.*'

'Granny is watching me. I'll remember!' Slightly called over her shoulder as she skipped out the door. By the time she'd reached the cab in the front drive, she'd forgotten all about it.

The trip through the elegant streets of the West End was soon over. Before they even rounded the corner, they could see the crowds had already gathered. The driver pulled up at the wrought-iron gates of the Hunterian Museum and Slightly forgave Mr John some of his boasting.

It really was a most impressive building.

'Like a great, grand castle!' said Slightly enthusiastically.

Once inside, however, what amazed her most was the *variety* of things on display, jam-packed into every inch of space in the great vaulted rooms. There were complete collections of insects and mammals, nests and shells, fossils of every size. There were musical instruments beside surgical instruments next to scientific instruments. Minerals, mummies, paintings, books, silver, fine china. And statues and maps and . . . it was dizzying!

'How can they even *tell* when something's stolen?' Slightly whispered to Mr Malcolm.

The Captain Cook knife was displayed in a small

glass cabinet of its own, and was receiving a lot of attention. It was surrounded by a buzzing, jostling crowd, everyone trying to get a look. Eventually Slightly and Mr Malcolm managed to work their way through to the front.

The knife was about a foot long, with a black obsidian blade and a dark, slightly greasy-looking wooden handle. Slightly felt a little disappointed. *What were you expecting – blood dripping off the end?* she scolded herself. *Besides, it's the thief you're interested in, not the bait!*

They moved to a better vantage point. Slightly's eyes darted back and forth, trying to spot a villain among the throng.

'He could be anywhere in the crowd, getting the lay of the land,' she murmured to Mr Malcolm. 'Keep your eyes peeled for a man with a peg leg!'

'Though anyone that clever is probably also a master of disguise,' replied Mr Malcolm. Slightly had to agree.

It was extremely frustrating to think that the person they wanted could be standing right in front of them and they wouldn't know it! It didn't matter how many times Slightly told herself to be patient – by the end of the afternoon she was so fed-up with being bumped into and having her toes trodden on while getting nowhere with the case that she was ready to scream!

'Excuse me, Miss Slightly?'

Her temper snapped like a twig! She spun round and demanded, '*What?*' so fiercely the speaker jumped back in alarm.

It was Mr John.

'Oh . . . I . . . oh,' said Slightly, turning beet red. 'I'm sorry. I . . .'

'Not at all,' said Mr John quickly. 'It was my fault for startling you. I only wished to invite you and my brother to the Trustees' Parlour. The trustees like to have a little snack at the end of the working day, and the Museum will be closing soon . . .'

The trustees' idea of 'a little snack' turned out to be the most sumptuous tea Slightly had ever seen, with dozens of delicate sandwiches and many different cakes and buns and fine China tea. Quiet servants moved about the room, keeping the fire well stoked, making sure everyone's cup was full, offering more and more to eat. There was a good deal of twittering amongst the trustees that no amount of cake and tea seemed able to calm, however. By practising the detective's art of eavesdropping, Slightly managed to overhear several different conversations about 'young Gentler's hare-brained scheme' and 'playing fast and loose with the Museum's reputation' and 'shocking, utterly unjustifiable risk' but whenever the old gentlemen noticed her listening they spluttered into their beards and changed the subject.

'Nobody here's going to believe it's actually *our* scheme – and it's not in the least bit "*hare-brained*"!' she muttered angrily to Mr Malcolm. 'And if one more old man calls me "little missy" and tries to pat me on the head like an infant, well, he better be prepared to lose some fingers, that's all.'

Mr Malcolm gave her a rueful smile. 'It isn't really the kind of group that appreciates girl detectives,' he said. 'Or musician sidekicks, for that matter.' Then he added, 'You know John will want to send you home pretty soon. Get you safely out of the way before they start laying the trap for the thief.'

'Send me home? Let him try,' snarled Slightly. She was in a thoroughly bad mood.

'I was thinking more in terms of staying out of the way so he *can't* try,' said Mr Malcolm mildly.

Hide and Seek! thought Slightly with a wicked grin. *I'm good at Hide and Seek!*

It was night, and all the well fed trustees had gone home, tutting to the last. In the great hall of the Hunterian Museum, Mr John and the head nightwatchman, Mr MacPherson, were deploying their troops.

'We will be concentrating our attention on the Captain Cook knife,' said Mr John. 'I will be concealed here, behind the polar bear. Mr MacPherson, as head of the watchmen, I'd like you there, between the antique Chinese map of the world and the mummy. Back against the wall, quite still . . . yes, you look just like an exhibit.' This made the under nightwatchmen giggle, for Mr MacPherson was a portly man and did look a little as if he'd been stuffed into his uniform.

Mr MacPherson rumbled, 'Yes, yes, very funny. When you've *quite* finished . . . Right, Fraser and Ross, you cover the upper galleries. MacDonald, the entrance hall. That's everything . . .'

'What about me?'

Mr John and Mr MacPherson turned in surprise. And there was Mr Malcolm, standing patiently beside a large kangaroo.

'Ah, Malcolm. I thought you went home with Miss Slightly?'

'No,' said Mr Malcolm with complete truthfulness.

'Ah.'

From her hiding place on the balcony, Slightly looked down and grinned. She could see that Mr

John was uncertain what to do with his brother.

She was lying on her tummy under a cabinet of pickled body parts. It was the perfect vantage point, but none of Mr John's official helpers would have been small enough to fit there.

'Sir, might I suggest posting the gentleman in the storeroom?' Mr MacPherson was saying. 'We'd feel pretty foolish if the thieves emptied *that* while we were stood round in here!'

Mr John looked relieved. 'Yes. Thank you. That's an excellent thought. Malcolm, Mr MacPherson will show you to your post.'

The two men climbed the stairs and headed for an insignificant-looking door at the back of the upper gallery. As they passed within a few inches of her, Slightly heard Mr MacPherson explaining, 'The storeroom's just along the corridor there. You see, sir, no matter how much we squeeze into the main halls, there's always too many things to display at one time. We've got something of everything in our storeroom, from beetles to books, surgical instruments to dinosaur bones. There's nothing under the sun that *somebody* won't take a mind to collect, and then they go and die and the son's wife, like as not, says, "I'm not having those dirty old things in *my* house!" and so it all just gets passed onto us . . .'

Poor Mr Malcolm, she thought, *banished to a dusty old storeroom when all the excitement is going to be out here!* It was unfair, but there was nothing she could do about it.

Mr MacPherson soon returned.

'Right – places, everyone!' ordered Mr John. 'Lights down.'

The gas was turned right down. As Slightly's eyes adjusted to the dimness, she saw the men settling themselves at their posts.

And the vigil began.

Slightly knew that this was something all detectives had to be good at. Waiting for the criminal to appear, keeping quiet, being invisible and alert . . . secretly she'd always thought it couldn't really be all that difficult.

It turned out to be very difficult indeed. She sighed and it sounded like a shout in the silence. Her right foot started to itch intolerably and she wriggled her toes to try to scratch them against the inside of her shoe – but she did it too hard and managed to kick the leg of the cabinet with a clunk. Then her nose itched. Moving her hand as slowly as possible, she reached up and scratched it. Even that sounded loud.

Time passed slowly. Minutes, hours – it was impossible to tell.

Slightly was right in the middle of an enormous silent yawn when she saw a flicker of movement out of the corner of her eye. She froze with her mouth wide open. (Then she heard Granny's voice in her head saying, 'I'm watching you' and shut it again.)

Mr MacPherson had neglected to close the door to the corridor behind her and she could see something moving there in the shadows. For a horrible moment she wondered if Mr Malcolm had nodded off and was sleepwalking again. But then she realised *she was seeing two shapes* in the dimness.

Two shapes and a strange *tap, tap* . . .

Chapter Seven:
Into the Night!

As silently as possible, Slightly squirmed out from under the cabinet and crept over to peer into the corridor. The gas was turned down so low she could barely see but she was sure there was something definitely *wrong* about the intruders. Why were they shaped like that? Too short. All hunched over and odd.

Tap, tap.

Creak . . .

They vanished into the storeroom.

And the moment they were out of sight, Slightly realised who they were: the one-legged man and the thieving ape! In the same room as poor Mr Malcolm! What might they do to him? She strained her ears. Was that the sound of a struggle? A muffled cry for help? The silence stretched out. Maybe he was well enough hidden . . . Maybe they hadn't noticed him . . .

Creak.

The two figures reappeared. They were laden down with bundles, but nothing that looked like a lifeless Mr Malcolm. Still, Slightly had to be sure.

She waited until the thieves had disappeared down the corridor, then rushed over to the storeroom door and stuck her head in.

'Mr Malcolm?' she whispered. 'Are you all right?'

'Yes . . . no – I'm stuck behind this cabinet . . .' It was a relief to hear his voice. 'Did you see them?'

There was no time to help Mr Malcolm. He would have to unstick himself.

'Don't worry!' she called softly over her shoulder. 'I'm on the trail!'

There was a muffled, 'No! Wait!' from the storeroom, but Slightly was already scurrying away.

At the end of the corridor she came to a staircase, leading into the depths of the Museum. On tiptoe, she skittered down, following the furtive sounds below.

Tap, tap.

The corridor she arrived in was cold and musty-smelling. There was no fine polished mahogany or marble here, just bare flagstones and whitewashed walls. She was in the basement, the realm of the Museum's army of servants.

Tap, tap.

In the darkness Slightly saw there was a bar of light showing under one of the doors. She crept closer and slowly, painstakingly, eased the door open a crack.

She was peering into a pantry with a counter and a sink, and containers for food. The room must only be partly underground, she realised, because there was a window above the counter. It was open.

But where were the one-legged man and the beast? All she could see was a boy and a girl. The girl was leaning on a crutch, then she shifted to one side and the crutch hit the stone floor with a woody *tap* . . . and Slightly realised her mistake! What a fool she'd been! There was no sunburnt, mad-eyed, crocodile-maimed criminal, no hairy, bloody-fanged ape – just a couple of ragged street children . . .

. . . who were handing bundles of swag through the window to someone outside. Quick as a flash, the boy climbed up and out after them, but the girl with the crutch was clumsier. As she clambered onto the counter she knocked over one of the pottery crocks, scattering flour everywhere.

'Milly?' came an anxious whisper from outside.

'Don't fuss. I'm coming,' the girl hissed back, and dragged herself through the window.

Slightly lunged forward, up onto the counter and quickly stuck her head out of the opening. The thieves were already hurrying along the side of the Museum towards the street.

Pausing only long enough to draw an arrow in the spilled flour, pointing to the window to show the others which way she'd gone, Slightly scrambled out after them.

Her feet had barely touched the ground when she heard, behind her, a horrible clanging sound – someone must have set off the Museum's alarm system.

Slightly groaned, convinced that the robbers would disappear now for sure.

But she was wrong.

They might not be as exotic as she'd imagined, but these thieves were obviously *experienced*. Nothing attracts attention like running away, and Slightly was impressed at the way they calmly dawdled along the gutter, as if completely unconcerned by the racket behind them.

She counted three of them now – a tall boy, a short boy and the tiny girl with the crutch. They were dirty and their clothes were ragged and, in spite of the cold, none of them had shoes. They couldn't have looked less like criminal masterminds if they'd tried. Trotting at their heels was a small white dog of indeterminate breed. It must have been waiting outside with the tall boy.

They were heading north. Slightly set off after them, keeping a careful distance, while also checking back over her shoulder for Mr Malcolm or Mr John or the nightwatchmen to appear.

She wondered what was keeping them. *We're going to lose the thieves if they don't get here soon!*

But suddenly, she realised that that was exactly what had happened. While she'd been gawking over her shoulder, the gang had disappeared, right at a junction with another road!

Which way had they gone? Slightly was beside herself. She could tell it was getting on for late, but there were plenty of cabs and pedestrians still about, making it even harder to see her quarry. Had they continued north? Had they turned left? Or right?

Frantically she craned her neck, peering in every direction.

And then she had some luck. There, down the

road to the right, just whisking away between the legs of the passers-by, she caught a glimpse of the wriggly white shape of the dog.

Yes! Slightly crowed – and then, for a brief moment, she hesitated. If she went any further, her friends would have no idea where she was. They couldn't possibly catch up with her if they didn't know which way she'd gone.

But maybe the thieves weren't going far. Surely they weren't working alone? Maybe they were planning to meet the *real* criminal mastermind just a little way away – she could track them to his lair, and *then* come back and tell the others. How unprofessional it would be if she stopped now and then they turned into a house or something half a minute further on! No good detective would let that happen. *She* wouldn't let that happen.

Slightly dashed forward, running dangerously through the night-time traffic, ignoring the angry shouts of the cab drivers and the snorting of the horses.

Now that they were well away from the Museum, the little group had picked up the pace. They showed no sign of stopping, either, or turning into any of the houses or shops along the way.

Where are you going? Slightly worried to herself and then, *Oh, no!*

Ahead she could see the black slash in the earth that marked the opening to Glasgow's great engineering project . . . the Underground. Miles of tunnel that would wrap around the city, that would soon be filled with trains and lights and passengers.

But not yet. Now it was empty, dark, damp.

And the thieves were heading straight for it.

Slightly's throat tightened. *No, please! Not down there!*

For a moment the thieves hesitated at the top of the steep, muddy slip road and Slightly's panic eased a little. She was close enough now to see there was a guard's makeshift hut at the bottom of the trench and a barricade of trestles blocking off the open mouth of the tunnel. The guard himself was leaning against the barrier smoking a pipe and he looked set to be there for some time. But then suddenly a squall of rain swept in! With a curse, he hunched his shoulders and ducked into the hut. Immediately the thieves scuttled forward, slipped past the trestles and forward into the darkness of the tunnel beyond.

What do I do? What do I– No time . . .

Crushing the terrifying thought that now none of her friends would *ever* be able to find her, Slightly gathered her courage in both hands and followed them . . .

Two steps into the tunnel and the damp coldness hit her and a horrifying fear of losing her way underground swelled up inside her so hard and so fast that she very nearly cried out. She had already turned round and was about to push her way out again before she managed to get a grip.

Stop it, Slightly, stop it! She struggled to calm down. *That's just stupid – it's a tunnel – it goes in a straight line – it's impossible to get lost in a tunnel!*

And it wasn't *completely* dark. When she turned back to look, she could see dim gaslight showing some distance ahead and, even as she watched, her little gang of thieves hurried under it and on into the next section. Now that they had passed the guard they weren't taking such care to walk silently. It was likely the noise they were making would cover her own footsteps. For a moment she wanted to just pretend she hadn't seen them – that they'd escaped her and she could turn back – but she put the thought behind her.

With a gulp, she followed the thieves.

It was a nightmare. In between the widely spaced pools of gaslight, it was impossible to see. She had to go by feel, one hand along the dripping wall, her feet slipping about on the greasy mud.

Oh, Matthew! she thought suddenly with a quiet

whimper. *I wish you were here!* If only she were holding his hard, dirty, cold hand, she knew she'd feel so much braver.

Though she also knew he'd be even more unbearably smug than he was already, if he ever discovered she'd been thinking like that! *But Mr Holmes has Dr Watson!* Matthew would make a terrible Dr Watson – he couldn't even write yet! Anyway, *he'd* want to be Mr Holmes.

Well, she wasn't having that! Gritting her teeth (which had started to chatter with the cold), Slightly staggered on, a shadow in the darkness. A shadow who kept slipping and almost falling over! She managed to catch herself each time, but then she twisted her ankle on a loose rock, landed on her hands and knees and couldn't help but cry out a little. Luckily it was too small a noise to be detected by human ears – but a dog's ears were something else again!

With an enquiring yap, the little white shape detached itself from the group ahead and trotted back. Straight towards her.

Slightly froze on her hands and knees in the cold mud, hardly daring to breathe.

The little dog nosed around her, growling softly. *Danger? Dinner?* Then, with a sneeze, he made up his mind. *Unimportant.*

'Ratbane! Where are you? Here, boy!' A boy's whisper came out of the darkness ahead, and the little dog bustled off towards it.

'Hurry up, Kenny,' another low voice called. 'There's no time to waste!'

Phew! Slightly let out her breath in a whoosh. She got back onto her feet, tried to brush herself down, succeeded in spreading mud further over her dress, and hobbled off once more.

She fixed her eyes on the next pool of light. What else could she do? But it felt as if the tunnel had no end. It felt as if she'd been underground for hours and hours.

Hours and hours, she began to repeat to herself, *and hours and hours and . . .*

Suddenly, Slightly gasped. The group ahead came under the gaslight again and it had changed! A new figure had joined them, a grotesque, misshapen, hunchbacked form that loomed threateningly over the others.

Their evil master! Slightly was sure that's what she was seeing. *And he isn't even human! He's . . . he's a monster. A demon!* In her mind she saw an image of a horrible, black-hearted creature whose inner evil had infected his body, deformed and ghastly to look at, capable of who knows what dire deeds . . .

Then the figure stepped more fully into the light and Slightly went limp with relief as she realised how silly she'd been. It was nothing more sinister than the big boy taking the girl with the crutch up onto his shoulder to carry her.

Of course! I knew that, she told herself firmly over the noise of her frantically beating heart, but it was a moment before she could regather her courage enough to continue. And in that moment, her quarry had moved on.

She started after them, then began a shuffling run as she realised there was something different up ahead. Something new. At long last, the section of tunnel they'd been following was coming to an end.

Though she wasn't aware of it, Slightly was grinning all over her grimy face.

The thieves had already squirmed through the barrier and were heading up the muddy slip road. They didn't look back. The rain had stopped and the moon was just past full, giving enough light to see that here, too, the guard preferred the shelter of his hut to keeping watch in the chilly outdoors.

Slightly ran up out of the pit. Tenement buildings loomed on every side, and her quarry was moving into a narrow alley between two of them. She nipped in after them – and started to gag.

'Aaarghh!' she croaked, covering her nose and mouth with her hands.

Sewage, stagnant pools of dirty water, dead rats – the things that festered in the gutters and against the walls were rank with the stench of poverty and neglect.

She tried not to breathe in too deeply.

Suddenly a man lurched out of the shadows and grabbed her arm.

'Hello, sweetheart, what's a pretty little girl like you doing out all alone?'

She could smell the beer on his breath and the stink of mould and old sweat from his clothes. Fear gave her a sudden burst of strength and she wrenched herself away, ripping her sleeve in the process and causing the big man to stagger, his feet slipping in the filth.

He swore at her as she fled, the words blurred by drink and his thick accent. Down the alley she ran and out into a wider street. Hard, starved faces stared at her from doorways. Bedraggled women and scarecrow men hung about the boiled pudding carts and dilapidated coffee stalls, or wandered drunkenly across the road. There were barefoot, rickety children too, scrounging in the gutters and dodging grown-ups. But none were *hers*.

Where are they? she thought, panicking, looking left and right. She was horrified at the thought of being lost here – it was more frightening even than the tunnel – but once again her luck held.

The little dog, Ratbane, had stopped to sniff round the wheels of the cats' meat man long enough for Slightly to catch sight of him. Satisfied with his inspection, he turned east again and trotted purposefully on.

Yes! Now she had the children in her sights again, Slightly hurried to close up the gap. They scurried past the great bulk of the cathedral, down into a gully and up the other side, then along the base of a high railing – Slightly caught glimpses of gravestones beyond. The thieves were moving faster now, as if confident of their ground, or perhaps because they were almost at their destination . . .

Then, without warning they reached a clump of bushes, and disappeared. Slightly waited for a moment. Nothing happened. Against every instinct, she went closer. Even in the moonlight it was hard to see, but by crouching down, she found a place where she could creep under the dripping branches. Water trickled icily down her neck, making her shudder uncontrollably. Bent in half, hands outstretched, she shuffled forward. There was definitely a path under the bushes, well used, like an animal trail. When it reached the railing, someone had dug a shallow trench under it. Only a small person would be able to squeeze through.

Don't think, Slightly. Don't think. Just do it.

She was panting hard as she stuck first her arms and then her head in, started to squirm forward – and froze. There, inches from her face, were six bare feet, five normal and one twisted . . .

Back! Go back!

It was too late. Before she could move a muscle, someone pulled a rank-smelling sack over her head. Claw-like fingers took hold of her and dragged her the rest of the way through the gap, ripping her dress and scraping the skin off her shins – and something, or someone, began to snarl . . .

Chapter Eight:

House of the Dead

Immediately, low-voiced squabbling broke out.

'We were *followed* – how could you be so careless?!'

'It was Gorbal's job to keep watch –'

'Nobody *said* it was my job! I thought *Kenny* was watching!' whined a hoarse voice.

'Oh, shut it. It's just a girl, anyway. Be *quiet*, Ratbane!'

'Shall I conk her on the head and dump her down the docks? There's good money in that dress.' It was the hoarse voice again.

A boy's.

'If Miss hears you talking like that, Gorbals, she'll dump *you* down the docks. Get her up and bring her along now.' That was the girl – Milly – the one with the crutch.

Someone dragged Slightly roughly to her feet. The sack smelled foul and made it hard to breathe. She could feel her head starting to spin.

She wanted to be brave, but she couldn't help a whimper escaping.

'We haven't got time for this – Gorbals, take the sack off her!'

'Wouldn't take no time to slit her throat a little,' grumbled the one called Gorbals, but he did as he was told.

Slightly felt the horrible rough jute sliding across her skin and blinked hard. The thieves she had been following for so long were standing there, looking at her. She took a deep breath of the cold, damp air, and then another. And then . . .

. . . she grabbed the small thief, shoved her towards the throat-slitting thief, who cannoned into the tall thief with the dog in his arms – and then she *scarpered*!

A forest of gravestones and monuments loomed up. Slightly darted between them, slipping on the wet grass, trying to see a path in the jumble of deep shadow and moonlight. A weird whistling sound came from behind her, which made her run even faster. It came again, this time from her right – from her left – she was being hunted!

A flicker of movement between the tombs ahead caught her eye and she tried to change direction. Her feet skidded, but she managed to squeeze through a gap between two stone angels. She started to run again – something white rose up in front of her – she screamed and tried to turn, but there were white things everywhere!

She was surrounded by ghosts. They were pale and shapeless and seemed to glow in the pale moonlight. She looked wildly from one to another . . . *No faces! They have no faces!*

And then someone grabbed her shoulder and spun her round.

It was Gorbals.

'Gotcha!'

There was a disgusted sound. 'Gorbals, you glaikit numpty – this is no place to be playing tig!'

And to Slightly's astonishment, the ghosts walked off, grumbling.

'Scared you, didn't they!' sniggered Gorbals. 'That's what's *supposed* to happen. We want the whole East End thinking the Necropolis is haunted!'

'The . . . the Necropolis?' quavered Slightly,

panting. 'This is the Necropolis?' She remembered Mr John speaking about the place, how his Jenny was buried there, but *he'd* said it was green and peaceful and pretty! 'Those weren't ghosts?'

'Tell her on the way.' It was the tall boy, Kenny, carrying the sacks, with Milly hobbling up behind him. 'Come on – Miss needs the things.'

They headed off, Gorbals keeping a tight grip on Slightly's arm.

'I'm Milly,' said the small thief. She was keeping up well, in spite of her crutch. 'Don't worry, that was just some patrol ghosts you saw. Miss organises them. Thinking there's ghosts and ghouls walking about keeps the worst of the rough ones from coming in here to kip, though if they get drunk enough they forget. We keep watch and try to scare them off before they get too far into the cemetery.'

'And the filthy resurrection men are feart and all!' said Kenny over his shoulder.

'Aye, and the police . . . mostly.'

Slightly's head was full of questions but she put them on hold. She needed to keep all her wits about her if she were ever to find her way out again! As they hurried further and further into the graveyard, she did her best to keep track of the twists and turns, tried to take note of landmarks like obelisks or angels showing white in the moonlight, a tree bare against the night sky – *anything* that might help her retrace her steps later. But it was hopeless. The thieves seemed to have eyes in their feet, and the path they followed was like a secret track in a forest that only the wild creatures knew.

Where are we going? she wailed silently. *What kind of a cemetery* is *this – it's the size of a city! How will I ever get out again?*

And, small and insistent at the back of her mind, a little voice kept saying, *They'll never find you, your friends will never, ever find you . . .*

And then, for no reason Slightly could see, the thieves stopped.

They had come to a halt before the dark door of a mausoleum – a house for the dead. It had been constructed to look like a proper building, with Greek columns and a great, heavy, metal door – a scaled-down version of a fine municipal building like a bank, or even a museum. It must have been an impressive place in its day, but it was smothered in ivy now. It looked as if no one had visited it in years.

The tall thief – Kenny – stepped up to the door and gave an odd triple knock on the metal. For a moment there was silence . . .

. . . and then something truly creepy happened.

Slightly heard a heavy bolt being drawn back . . . *from inside the tomb*. Slowly grating across the stone with a sound that made her skin crawl, the great iron door was opening.

And then she knew why she'd been brought here. All that talk about pretend ghouls and ghost patrols had just been to fool her. She knew what was really in that tomb – she could see them clearly in her mind – she'd been brought as prey for the Living Dead! She could picture them gathering, eagerly, behind the door, their bones showing through their tattered shrouds, lurching closer and closer, reaching out with their ghastly fingers to draw her in – there would be worms curling out of their eye sockets – she just knew there would be worms –

Oh, Granny! Goodbye forever! she thought desperately and shut her eyes tight.

'What kept you?' said a voice. It came from somewhere at a level with Slightly's knees.

She opened her eyes and looked down into a child's face. It was grubby, certainly, but unmistakably still alive and uninfested. She felt a wave of relief – *No worms! I'm so glad there are no worms!* – then she was pushed forward through a hanging curtain of ivy and down some steep steps into the strangest place she had ever seen.

The inside of the mausoleum was one large rectangular room, like a great box. There was a sarcophagus opposite the door, several stone coffins placed on either side, and deep stone shelves stacked three or four high around the walls, designed to take the coffins of less important members of the family. And, wherever Slightly looked, there were two sorts of things she would never have expected to find in a tomb – living, breathing children, and a bewildering collection of artefacts!

There were ragged children gathered around the sarcophagus, laying it like a table with fine porcelain plates, pewter mugs, silver forks and knives. Some tended a fire on the stone floor where an antique bronze kettle on a trivet was just starting to steam. Instead of coffins on the shelves, there were beds of bracken with children looking sleepily out. And everywhere Slightly's eyes were caught by glints of colour: gold from a serene-looking Buddha; jewel-like blues and greens from paintings of the seaside; the warm fur tones of a stuffed marmot and the mellow wood of a lute; a rich tapestry hung beside a stack of cheap pine coffins; blue bits of stone, and jade carvings, and maps, and a Japanese fan . . .

As Slightly stared about in amazement, a picture of Limpopo House came suddenly into her mind, and she understood. The things that were stolen from the Museum . . . they were stolen to make a *home*! There was no pagan ritual. No one-legged beast master. There was only a bunch of street children, not doing any harm to anybody, just trying to live in a tomb!

She had a horrible, overwhelming vision of policemen breaking in on this strange domestic scene – Milly and the others being arrested as thieves – Mr John saying, 'Well done, Slightly! Now we've caught the evil miscreants, we can properly punish them!' and calmly ticking each artefact off his list as the children were dragged away in tears . . .

There was a horrible, tight, guilty feeling in her chest.

'Bonny, isn't it!' said Milly proudly, and then turned to the others. 'Where's Miss?'

'She's with Sandy,' someone replied. 'She's put him in her bed and is just waiting for you lot to get back so's she can operate on him.'

'Operate?!' exclaimed Slightly, jerked out of her miserable thoughts. 'What do you mean?'

'It's our Sandy,' explained Milly. 'He was in Cathedral Street and he slipped under a cart and it broke his leg something horrible. There's no money for the hospital, so Miss is going to do it. She sent us to the Museum as soon as it was dark to get the equipment she'll need. Museum's got a collection of *everything*, she said, and she was right.'

'She . . . *what*?' Slightly couldn't believe her ears – they had been stealing medical equipment!

'Miss works in the Museum, so she knows where everything is stored, and before she was a nurse, so she'll know how to use the stuff. Miss can do *anything*,' Milly said with a loving confidence shining from her pinched little face.

That was when Slightly decided. It didn't matter who this Miss was, or what she'd done. As soon as it was morning, somehow or other Slightly would find her way back to Granny and the others, and she would say she'd lost the thieves in the night and she had no idea where they'd gone. And as soon as Granny was well, they'd go home to Limpopo House and she'd never, never, *ever* stick her nose where it had no business again.

Just then, a baby started to cry. Slightly looked about, startled, but couldn't see one anywhere . . . until Milly bustled over to a coffin in the corner.

'Hush, Rottenrow, or you'll be waking the others,' she said.

Slightly followed, leaned over the edge of the coffin, and *stared*. Instead of a skeleton in a shroud, she saw three babies, wrapped in shawls, tucked into nests of straw. Two were sleeping peacefully and one was red-faced and fractious.

Milly picked the girning one up and began to joggle him.

'Hush, Rottenrow, you noisy boy,' she scolded softly. 'Hush now. You're teething, aren't you, poor mite.'

Slightly realised she was still staring. She cleared her throat and asked, 'So . . . er . . . why is he called Rottenrow?'

Milly seemed surprised at the question. 'It's where he was found, of course. This is our wee Rottenrow, and that's Drygate and by rights *that* should be North Canalbank but Miss Loch put her foot down and said we'd call her Jane.'

'But you . . . they . . . they're sleeping in a *coffin*!'

'So they are. Nice and snug. Keeps out the draughts. They don't give nearly enough thought to caulking, these tomb builders.'

Maybe because dead people don't generally mind *a draught,* thought Slightly to herself before almost leaping out of her skin as the triple knock on the metal door sounded again, echoing horribly in the enclosed space. Kenny ran to pull back the bolt and drag the door open – and the most beautiful lady

Slightly had ever seen ducked under the ivy curtain and stepped in. She was tall and strong, with raven-wing hair and luminous blue eyes and the face of a warrior queen. She was in every way Slightly's idea of . . .

. . . a heroine. She looked exactly like a heroine.

'Kenny, Milly – you're back!' the lady cried. 'Thank goodness! Were you followed?'

Even her voice is beautiful! thought Slightly.

'Course not, Miss Loch. At least, well . . . there was her.'

Miss Loch gave Slightly a quick glance.

'She doesn't exactly look like a policeman, does she.'

Slightly looked down at her torn and muddied clothes. She looked like just another street child.

'*I* thought she was trouble. *I* thought we should get rid of her,' the one called Gorbals muttered huskily.

'You were wrong. There's always room in a tomb,' said the lady. She smiled and Slightly's heart gave a weird twitch. But the lady's attention quickly turned back to the thieves. 'Well? Did you find the things I need?'

'Yes, I think so, Miss.'

Slightly was extremely curious to see the swag she'd been following through the night. The thieves dumped a gruesome collection of medical equipment – forceps and spreaders and saws and blades – out onto the sarcophagus. Just the sight of them made Slightly cringe a little. But Miss Loch seemed quite at home with this sort of weaponry. She looked them over quickly, selected some of the most fearsome and handed them to one of the girls.

'I want these boiled up in the cleanest pot we've got – that's a good rolling boil, mind, not just a simmer.' She turned back to the scroungers. 'And the carbolic sprayer?'

'It weren't easy to find, Miss,' said Milly. 'Right at the back of the case. But I'm pretty sure this is it.' And she opened another sack and carefully drew out a . . . thing. It was a squat black metal contraption with a wooden handle on one side, metal tubing and a glass vial on the other side. Slightly had absolutely no idea what it might be for, but Miss Loch was delighted.

'Milly, you're a treasure. God bless Dr Lister! It may not be modern, but with this I think we've got a chance. Now I need some completely clean hands – hurry!'

There was a general scrum around the washing bucket. Unsure what else to do, Slightly went with the others. When her turn at the bucket came, a part of her mind noticed that the tomb-dwellers had the use of some of the fine soap she'd seen in the Trustee's marble washroom just that day. When she'd used it last she'd been sure the thieves were evil, an adversary to be outsmarted and overcome. Now . . .

The horrible feeling in her chest welled up again. She gulped and stood in line with the others, holding out her hands as they did.

Miss Loch came down the line, briskly checking fingers and nails in a way that made Slightly think of Granny. When she came to Slightly, however, she stopped suddenly.

'Here, these aren't gutter hands! Who are you?' But before Slightly could think what to answer the lady shook her head. 'No time – you can tell me your story later. All I need to know now is, are you squeamish?'

She looked at Slightly . . . and something huge happened. If the lady had sprouted flaming wings on the spot, or suddenly leapt onto a white steed ready to take on the world, the feeling inside Slightly couldn't have been stronger. All at once she wanted – more than anything – for Miss Loch to call *her* 'a treasure'. It didn't matter that she was a complete stranger. It didn't matter that she was the leader of a band of thieves, or that she apparently ate her meals off someone else's sarcophagus, or kept babies in a coffin. All that mattered was that Slightly wanted her approval. Badly.

'I . . . I . . .' she stuttered, and then more firmly, 'No, I'm not squeamish.'

Miss Loch's blue eyes widened. 'Not a gutter voice, either!' she said. 'And your name?'

'Slightly.'

'Right, Slightly, we'll talk when the job's done. Meantime, we need more light – bring these candlesticks. Milly, you come after with the instruments when they're ready – get Gorbals and Kenny to carry the pot.'

She gathered up the sprayer, and Slightly followed her out into the night, round the back of the tomb, and up to the entrance of another, smaller, hexagonal mausoleum, wreathed like the first in dense overgrowing ivy.

'It's Miss!' the lady called out. 'Let me in!'

I wonder who lives here? thought Slightly, and then made a face at herself. How quickly she'd got used to the idea of people living in tombs at all!

The door scraped open, and a small, anxious face peered out.

'Miss? Thank goodness you're here. He's . . . I think he's passed out.' Then the girl spotted Slightly and frowned. 'Who's that?'

'She's new,' said Miss Loch. 'And she has clean hands. Off you go, Hetty my dear, and let us fix your brother, all right?'

'Oh, Miss . . .' and the little girl's eyes welled up. The tears made white marks down her dirty face. 'Don't send me away!'

Miss Loch gave her a long look, and then nodded. 'If I show you how to drip chloroform onto this cloth, would you be able to keep him under? It'll take a steady hand.'

Immediately, the little girl scrubbed the tears off her face with her sleeve and stood straight.

'Thank you, Miss. You can count on me, Miss.'

So this is her tomb – I mean, room, thought Slightly, peering about curiously.

It was small and bare. There was a boy, motionless on Miss Loch's bed, which was made of a pile of bracken and ragged blankets, on top of the single sarcophagus that took up most of the space. Then, as Miss Loch lit more candles, Slightly saw that here, too, the Museum had provided some ornament.

There was one small painting, leaning on a rough shelf. It showed mostly darkness, except where a group of people were clustered around a body in the light. She remembered writing the words into her notebook as Mr Malcolm read off the list: *Oil sketch by Rembrandt, oak panel, 30 by 40 inches.*

Miss Loch noticed her staring at it. 'Beautiful, isn't it? Milly got it for me as a birthday present. I keep meaning to make her take it back, and then changing my mind!'

'Er . . .' said Slightly, uncertain what to say, but Miss Loch was already rolling up her sleeves.

'Now, let's see if I can get Dr Lister's machine to work,' she said.

She began to fiddle about with the spraying machine, filling it with strong-smelling carbolic acid. The first few times she worked the handle the liquid came out in acrid splats, but after a while she was able to produce a fine mist instead. By the time she had it working reliably, Kenny and Gorbals arrived with the sterilised instruments in the pot.

'Just put those down. Gorbals, wait outside in case I need something else fetched. Kenny, you go and make sure the others are all right,' said Miss Loch. Slightly noticed how grateful both boys looked to be getting out of the sick room! She stood up a little straighter, even more determined not to let Miss Loch down.

'Hetty, remember what I told you,' Miss Loch was saying. 'A drop of the chloroform and then count slowly. We mustn't send him down too deep, or let him come round. Milly, keep the sprayer going. No matter how uncomfortable it makes us feel, I want carbolic spray on everything and everyone.'

Hetty placed the cloth over her brother's nose and mouth, let a little of the chloroform onto it, and began to count. Slightly shuddered at the smell of the fumes. Milly worked the sprayer, covering them all in a choking carbolic mist that made their throats and eyes itch and their skin burn.

'Good. Now, Slightly, you stand here. I want you to put your hands round his knee, like this, and hold it steady. I'm going to pull from his foot here. I need to realign the bones. Look away if you have to, but hold tight!'

Even with Miss Loch's permission, Slightly found she *couldn't* look away. It was horrible and fascinating. The way the white jagged bone stuck out of the boy's flesh – the dark blood and the purple bruising – the way he moaned, even while unconscious, as Miss Loch dragged back on his foot and twisted – it was awful. At the same time, she couldn't take her eyes off the way Miss Loch was taking the disaster that was Sandy's leg and bringing it back from the brink. She cleaned, and realigned, and stitched, and splinted until everything that could be done had been done, and it was up to the body's healing powers to do the rest.

'That's it, then,' said Miss Loch at last. 'There's nothing more I can do.'

There was a breathless pause.

'Will he be all right?' asked Slightly anxiously.

'I think so,' said Miss Loch. 'Yes. I hope so. He'll sleep now, and that's the best thing for him.' Still she stood there, looking down at the boy, as if unable to move a muscle now that the crisis was over.

'Come away then, Miss,' said Milly, taking charge. 'Hetty will watch him, and Gorbals will stay too. He'll run and fetch you the second you're needed. You said Sandy'll sleep now and you should do the same. You can rest on my shelf. Come away, now, there's a good Miss.'

Slightly bundled the instruments and bottles and bloody cloths into the pot, picked it up and followed Milly as she led Miss Loch out of the tomb.

'It's still night!' Miss Loch murmured. 'I thought it must be morning.'

Slightly was surprised too. Had they been about their work for so short a time? She was utterly weary – it had felt like weeks!

Milly gave the special knock at the door of the main tomb and immediately it was dragged open.

Everyone clustered forward as they came in. Slightly was the last one to enter. Because her arms were full, she pushed the door shut with her behind and then was gathered into the crowd of questioners.

'Is Sandy all right?'

'Did you do it, Miss?'

'Will he keep his leg?'

'Will he die?'

Miss Loch stumbled into the middle of the tomb and leaned against the sarcophagus.

'He'll be fine,' she said. 'God willing. He's . . .' Then, abruptly, she stopped. She was listening intently. 'Shush!' she whispered. 'I thought . . . I thought I heard something . . .'

Everyone froze. Then, from outside the tomb, it came again. The sound of voices, men's voices, urgent or angry, and far, far too close.

'Who's on patrol?' whispered Miss Loch – but no one was. Everyone was already *here*, come to hear the news about their friend. No one had been on guard.

And then it got worse.

'No,' whispered Milly. 'The door's not barred!'

Before anyone could move, it was too late. Ratbane started to growl, but Kenny grabbed hold of him and clamped his hand tight over his muzzle. The door began to grate inwards. There had been no reassuring, secret knock. Slightly's heart was pounding in her chest. Violent drunks, resurrection men, bent coppers ... what kind of men were breaking in? What could they do? There was nowhere to hide, no help. They couldn't even run away – they were caught in a trap! The children huddled together, too frightened to make a noise. Miss Loch grabbed a branched silver candlestick and brandished it like a flaming sword, sending spatters of wax onto the stone floor. Slightly looked about wildly for a weapon of her own but before she could find anything the door had opened and ...

Chapter Nine:
The Intruders

. . . Mack the dog woofled in!

Ratbane immediately exploded into a hysteria of barking, leaping out of Kenny's arms and dancing madly around the intruder dog, stiff-legged, hackles up. Mack paid no attention. Tail waving, *he* padded over to Slightly, licked her hand and collapsed across her feet.

'SLIGHTLY? WHERE ARE YOU?'

Mr Malcolm and Mr John stumbled down the steps, looking about wildly. The noise from Ratbane echoed horrendously but Slightly, still pinned by the weight of Mack, shouted her loudest, '*I'm here! It's all right. I'm all right!*'

Mr Malcolm rushed over and hugged her, hard.

'We found you! You're all right! John, she's all right!'

But Slightly could see that Mr John wasn't even looking in her direction. He had stopped in his tracks and was staring like a man who has suddenly, unexpectedly, seen a vision.

He was staring at Miss Loch.

Slightly looked too, and her heart gave that strange twitch again.

Miss Loch stood there, drawn up to her full height, her black hair escaped entirely from its pins and tumbled around her shoulders, the light from the candles glowing on her skin. Slightly could see from her eyes that she was afraid and angry and ready to do battle for her family . . . tired out, tattered, with Sandy's blood on her blouse, she was every inch a heroine! Mr John couldn't take his eyes off her.

But then he made a big mistake. He took a step towards Miss Loch – and the terror that had so far held her ragged children frozen like a spell suddenly snapped. Shrieking in chorus, they threw themselves at Mr John, knocked him onto the floor and buried him in a heap of biting and scratching!

With a roar, Mr Malcolm rushed to his brother's rescue, plucking first one flailing child and then another off of him. Miss Loch said something that was probably unladylike and waded in as well. Mack was growling uncertainly but Slightly threw her arms around his neck and held on tight.

Never before or since had the quiet of a tomb been so entirely shattered!

Then, almost as suddenly as it started, the uproar was over. Mr John staggered to his feet, his hair a mess, his tie under one ear, his coat ripped and a scratch on his cheek that was starting to bleed a little. Miss Loch stepped back, breathing heavily, and Slightly eased her stranglehold on Mack.

There was a moment of unbearable tension.

Say something! Slightly urged herself, but before she could think where on earth to start, Miss Loch spoke instead.

'I give you fair warning, Mr John Gentler – if you try to harm my children I will kill you.'

Granny always said that it was better to get right to the point than to waste time beating about the bush. Still . . . *I'm not sure I would have started there!* thought Slightly, and certainly she had never seen anyone quite as discombobulated as Mr John at that moment.

'Harm children? Kill me?' he spluttered, and then, '*How do you know my name?*'

'Is he safe, Miss?' interrupted Kenny.

'Are you, sir?' Miss Loch demanded, never taking her eyes off Mr John. 'Are you safe? Do I have your word?'

Mr John straightened his tie and squared his shoulders. 'If you know me, as you seem to, you would know that I have never harmed a child in my life,' he said, 'and I have no intention of starting now. You have my word.'

'He's safe,' Miss Loch announced with a nod.

At her words there was a general sigh of relief. Slightly smiled as little Milly hobbled over to Mr John and tried to brush some of the dirt off him. He looked down at her in a vague way but his attention was still focused on Miss Loch.

'But this is unbelievable – please, you must tell me – *how do you know who I am?* I don't understand! I know I would remember meeting you!'

'Really?' Miss Loch's voice was icy. 'You would remember meeting a servant? You'd remember meeting someone who poured your tea and carried in the coal and cleaned the stairs? I think it's unlikely, Mr John Gentler. Everyone knows servants are invisible.'

'I don't understand,' repeated Mr John.

'Miss works at the Museum, mister,' explained Kenny helpfully. 'She cleans and such.'

'And Mr John Gentler is a trustee of the Hunterian Museum,' said Miss Loch, 'from which so many items have lately disappeared.' She sounded suddenly weary to Slightly.

'Oh, but it weren't Miss Loch, mister,' Milly piped up. '*She* never stole a thing from you. That was us and all. And it was only little stuff. Well, we couldn't get big stuff out the pantry window, could we?'

'Shush, Milly!' cried Miss Loch.

The situation was going from bad to worse. All Slightly wanted was to get Mr John out of the tomb and away from here – away from the children and Miss Loch, before he found out too much and had to have them all arrested! A vision of Miss Loch in a prison cell rose in her mind – like Newgate, or worse! She couldn't let that happen! She disentangled herself from Mr Malcolm and Mack, and tried to push through the children to get to Mr John.

'Please – Mr John – I want to go home!' she called, but Milly was still chattering away.

'Miss draws us pictures, see, of what we need to nick and tells us where they're kept and she always keeps that window in mind.' It was obvious the little girl was quite taken with Mr John, looking up at him with shining eyes and paying no attention to Miss Loch's attempts to silence her.

'Pictures?' said Mr John, puzzled.

'Seeing as how none of us can read. Well, except for Kenny – he can read a bit – but he's too big to get in.'

'Ratbane and I stand outside,' said Kenny. 'I hand the little ones in and out and keep watch for the polis.'

Mr John look bemused. 'Polis?'

Oh, Kenny, be quiet! Slightly implored him silently.

'Stop telling them!' Miss Loch wailed.

'That's right,' continued Milly regardless. 'But like I said . . .'

'MILLY WILL YOU BE QUIET!' cried Miss Loch in desperation. She had gone quite white and swayed where she stood.

Slightly couldn't think what was wrong with her. Miss Loch was pointing at Mr John with a hand that shook.

'It *wasn't* them,' she panted. 'It was me. Everything they stole was at my bidding. I . . . I . . .'

Mr John leapt forward just in time to catch Miss Loch as she fell. The night's work had finished off even her formidable strength.

'No! Help me! Is she dead?!' he wailed.

Slightly had never heard a grown man wail before – it made her squirm inside – but Miss Loch was not dead. She had only fainted.

'Didn't I say she needed to sleep?' tutted Milly. 'Bring her over here, mister. We'll put her to rest on my shelf.'

'She sleeps on a . . . a *coffin shelf*?'

'No, no, normally she's got a whole tomb of her own,' she reassured him. 'But Sandy's in her bed with a horrible broken leg and we can't possibly move him. Slide her in right here, mister, and with any luck she'll just go from her faint into a sleep – it's what she needs most, take my word.' And she covered the limp form of Miss Loch with a ragged blanket and smoothed back her black hair with a gentle hand.

'Slightly,' murmured Mr Malcolm, 'is there any food in this place?'

'Food?'

'Yes. This lot looks half-starved. Do they have any supplies at all?'

'I think so . . .'

So, while Mr John hovered anxiously by Miss Loch on the shelf and the children whispered among themselves, Slightly took Mr Malcolm to the back of the tomb where there was a makeshift store cupboard.

He rummaged a while and ended by bringing out everything, laying it on the sarcophagus they used as a kitchen table.

'Here – what are you doing? – that's to last the week!' protested a tyke who barely reached Mr Malcolm's waist.

'Don't worry, I'll replace it all with more and better!' he reassured the child, as he stoked up the fire and gave Slightly some elderly unidentifiable vegetables to chop.

'What are we making?' she asked, trying not to look too closely at what she was doing.

'Surprise Soup,' said Mr Malcolm, stirring the pot and watching for the boil. 'When I first came to London, before I found my feet and started getting jobs in theatre orchestras – before I found Limpopo House – Surprise Soup was something I made quite a lot. It's a simple recipe – you take every edible thing you can find, chop it into pieces and dump it in a pot!' He noticed the look on Slightly's face and shrugged. 'It's hot, and if you don't focus on the flavour, it passes for a meal. Keeps you going till things get better!'

'Hey, mister, that doesn't look half bad!' said Kenny.

'He's making it for Miss, you horrible gannet,' scolded Milly.

'Well,' Mr Malcolm smiled down at her, 'Miss first, at any rate. There'll be a taste left for the rest of you, though.' He lowered his voice. 'She'll have been denying herself to keep them fed, I wouldn't doubt,' he murmured to Slightly. He looked about, taking in the tapestries and art, the silver and the sacking and the cold stone, the children in their rags and the white ghost robes that hung by the door. He shook his head in wonder.

'This is a strange place you've stumbled on, Slightly. Strange indeed. A house of children in a house of the dead – a house of finery and poverty at one and the same time.' He pointed at the work they were doing. 'Scraps and offal and silver spoons.'

'It's strange, but it's their home,' said Slightly. *And I wish I knew what was going to happen to them all now!* she thought. She knew she didn't really mean it, but part of her wished Mr John had never found her. But she wasn't ready to talk to Mr Malcolm about that yet. Besides, it wasn't *his* fault!

'How *did* you find me?' she demanded suddenly.

Mr Malcolm laughed softly. 'It was all Mack's doing – we wouldn't have had a hope without his superlative nose! I didn't realise my brother had brought him along. He was tied up round the back of the Museum in case we needed him, and we certainly did! John and I set off after you as soon as I told them what had happened. Mr MacPherson and the others stayed behind – he was absolutely convinced it was all a ruse to let our guard down, you see, and that a dozen midgets were planning to clean out the place while our backs were turned!'

He smiled at Slightly's startled look. 'He has quite a devious mind, our Mr MacPherson, and his theory all along was that the Museum was being robbed by a gang of midgets. As it turns out, he was closer to the truth than we were!'

Then he stopped smiling. 'I'm so sorry, Slightly, that you had to do this on your own. It was stupid, of course, to think you'd just stand about – I know you, after all! – but I blame myself completely for letting you go, and John for making you angry beforehand so that you would think you had to prove yourself. John's been doing the same. Oh, Slightly, if anything had happened to you . . . !'

'Nothing did,' Slightly tried to reassure him.

'You must have been scared,' said Mr Malcolm. He was not ready to be let off the hook just yet.

'I was!' She couldn't help shivering a little as she thought of the chase across the city and the ghosts and Sandy's leg. Then the miserable guilty feeling came back and tears welled in her eyes . . .

Mr Malcolm quickly hugged her again.

'We'd have been here sooner,' he said ruefully, 'but we kept having to stop and convince nightwatchmen to unlock gates for us and let us through. Poor Mack was going mad having to wait all the time. *He* could have wriggled through the holes and tight places easily but we were much too big!'

At this point Mr John wandered over. 'Food?' he said. 'A good idea. They all seem half-starved. Especially . . .' and he let his eyes drift back to the shelf where Miss Loch lay.

'And in the meantime,' said Mr Malcolm to Slightly, 'please tell us what in heaven's name has been happening here!'

'Yes, do,' said Mr John.

So, as the Surprise Soup bubbled in the pot, and Miss Loch escaped her cares in sleep for a while, Slightly told them the story of her night.

At the end Mr John asked, 'But how could she have known how to fix the lad's leg like that?' His voice was full of wonder.

'Because she used to be a nurse.' Milly had come up beside them unnoticed. 'At the Glasgow Royal Infirmary, just by the cathedral there. Until . . .' and Milly's little face scrunched up in fury '. . . until they threw her out.'

'Miss Loch! Why?' cried Slightly, immediately indignant.

'For arguing with the doctors when they were wrong,' Milly snarled. 'There was a little girl and they wanted to cut her arm off and Miss thought it could be saved and, well, apparently she knocked down one of the surgeons . . .'

'Oh, how I wish I could have seen that!' cried Slightly, and then turned red, expecting Mr John to scold.

But Mr John just looked thoughtful.

'The day they sacked her,' Milly continued, 'with no letter, mind, so she could never get another nursing position, not *ever* – she was so upset, she said, she just walked and walked and ended up here. It was after dark and the gate was locked and then she found us.'

'But –' Slightly wanted to know more. She had a thousand questions, but Mr John suddenly stood up.

'We should check on the boy,' he said firmly. 'She'd want us to. Slightly, if you could show the way?'

'Aye,' said Milly with an approving nod. 'You do that, and I'll mind Miss.'

And so Slightly and the Gentlers and Mack the dog went quietly out into the pearly light of a misty dawn and round to the other house-tomb. They found Gorbals curled up at the threshold, fast asleep, oblivious to all the recent fuss. He had a look of such innocence on his dirty face that Slightly could hardly believe he'd been threatening to slit her throat only a few hours before. Carefully stepping past, they eased open the door and tiptoed down the steps.

Sandy lay on Miss Loch's bed, his sister asleep beside him. Slightly glanced at Mr John, wondering what he was thinking about the Rembrandt painting leaning so casually on the rough bit of the wall behind the children's heads, but he didn't mention it.

'Do you think the boy's all right?' he whispered instead.

Slightly crept up to feel Sandy's forehead. Although his face was pale, there was no sign of fever and his breathing was regular and deep. She adjusted his covers, and signed to the Gentlers to come away.

'Miss Loch's wonderful,' she said, once they were in the night air again. She was talking to both of them, but it was Mr John she wanted to hear.

I have to make him understand, she thought urgently. *He just CAN'T have her arrested!*

'She's saved that boy's life, for sure,' she went on.

'Remarkable,' murmured Mr John.

'It wouldn't be too far to say she's saved *all* their

lives, really – it's so dangerous on the streets, and they have no family to look after them, or shelter, or enough food.'

'Truly astounding,' he said.

'She isn't anything like an evil bad criminal mastermind, is she?' Slightly continued anxiously. 'You couldn't really find anybody *less* like an evil bad criminal mastermind . . .'

'A wonder.'

'It almost makes me wish we hadn't found her. I mean, it wouldn't be *such* a bad thing if she got away with it. Of course, she'd have to stop stealing from the Museum – I'm not saying she should be allowed to empty the place! – but I can't help wondering if maybe we should just, well, you know, forget . . . ?'

That got Mr John's attention.

'Forget?' he exclaimed, turning on her so suddenly she jumped back. '*Forget*?'

'Well, I . . . I didn't mean, of course . . . I . . .' stammered Slightly.

Before she could explain what she *did* mean, Kenny came up, Ratbane at his heels.

'Miss wants a word with you,' he said, looking at Mr John. 'Now.'

Chapter Ten:

Seeing Ghosts Can Change Your Life

They came back into the main tomb to find Miss Loch awake and eating Surprise Soup out of an antique bowl with a silver spoon.

She stood up immediately. 'How is he?' she asked anxiously.

Before Slightly could report on their patient, Mr John answered.

'He's sleeping,' he said. 'No fever. Your skill has saved his leg and very probably his life.'

Miss Loch gave a sigh of relief, but stayed standing.

'I want you to

know I meant what I said before,' she said. 'Well, not about killing you. But no matter what the children have said to you, you must listen only to *me*. You have to understand that every misdeed of theirs was at my bidding, and I am entirely and solely responsible.'

'I will listen to anything you have to say, if only you will sit down as you do so,' said Mr John earnestly. And he held Miss Loch's broken chair for her as if she were the finest lady in the fussiest parlour in all Glasgow. Slightly wondered if she noticed, and thought perhaps she did, for her pale face flushed.

Miss Loch took a deep breath, and began to speak. 'I understand Milly has told you the sorry tale of my uncontrolled temper, and how I came to be wandering the Necropolis that night. I remember I found it soothing and I was . . . I was tempted to stay forever. We are fragile vessels, Mr Gentler, and it is not difficult to break us beyond repair.'

Slightly saw how Mr John put out his hand as if to comfort her, then pulled it back at the last minute as if afraid of offending her.

'I have seen death many times,' Miss Loch continued. 'I am not afraid of it. But I *was* surprised when I started to see ghosts. Little, scurrying ghosts that peeped out at me from behind the headstones.'

'Tell him who the ghosts were, Miss!' chorused

the children. 'They were us, weren't they, Miss!'

'That's right. They were you. You see, Mr Gentler, the East End children came here at night to huddle in the lee of the tombs and hide from the violence of the streets. It was their pale little faces I saw. They were wet and cold and . . . and I lost my temper. Again.'

'You should have seen her!' crowed Kenny, and Slightly wished she had! 'Miss were a sight for sore eyes! She started tromping up and down, muttering about how the dead had roofs but we didn't and how it wasn't right and she wasn't having it and then she came up to this place, and you could tell nobody'd visited it for ages because it was all covered in ivy and, well, she just bashed at the lock with a stone until it fell off and she walked straight in . . . and here we are!'

'She made us our ghost robes too and set up the patrols, to keep the drunks and the bodysnatchers and the police away,' added Milly. 'She gave us *everything*.'

'And *they* gave *me* a reason to keep trying,' said Miss Loch to Mr John. 'When I saw there was a servant's job going at the Museum, I took it, but there was barely enough money from that to feed us all. What could we do? Nothing that was legal. So, after breaking and entering tombs, came thievery.'

'But Miss had all these *rules*,' grumbled Gorbals.

'That's right. I would not have my children stealing from folk as poor as themselves. And stealing from the rich, with their high walls and guard dogs and dozens of servants would be far too dangerous, and the penalties too harsh. The Museum, though, was something else again.'

Slightly wished with all her heart that Mr John might see it that way too, but she had her doubts.

'It's clever and all,' interrupted Milly. 'What happens is, last thing at night, Miss slips the latch on the pantry window. First thing in the morning, before anyone else gets in for work, she shuts it again. So by the time your sort have noticed something's walked, there's no sign of how it happened!'

'Except when you decided you'd nick that ink bottle and it spilled and there were prints of your club foot and crutch marks all over the place,' said Kenny scornfully.

Milly looked embarrassed. 'But it was so pretty, that bottle!' she muttered. 'And anyway, that was a *good* thing I spilled that ink – it put the trustees onto the wrong scent altogether!'

'I'm sorry. I don't understand,' said Mr John, puzzled.

'Miss told us how she'd overheard you all deciding

it was a peg-legged man and his wild beast that were doing the stealing. Imagination ain't the half of it! Just from my poor old club foot and crutch in the ink!'

'Oh . . . oh dear . . . I do apologise . . . I never meant . . .' Mr John was as deeply embarrassed as Slightly had ever seen him.

'Don't you worry, mister,' said Milly. 'I've been called all sorts because of this foot of mine but nothing that ever made me laugh before!' And she reached over and patted Mr John in a motherly way.

Miss Loch watched this exchange with a small smile, and continued her tale.

'At first I only thought of stealing coal for our fire. And leftover cakes, though there were rarely any of those.'

Slightly had a sudden, vivid picture in her mind of dozens of cakes disappearing into those greedy trustees.

'Then I started to think . . . we had a roof and four stone walls, but nothing else. I wanted . . . I wanted my girls and boys to have more.'

Slightly wondered what it could be that Miss Loch wanted for them.

Mr John was wondering as well.

'What more did you want them to have?' he asked.

Miss Loch looked straight at him, took a deep breath and said, 'I wanted them to have some beauty.' There was a pause, then, 'You must arrest me,' she added. 'I understand perfectly. It was very, very wrong, but that's the truth of why I did it. And now you know.'

The children stirred uneasily. Why was Miss talking about being arrested? Hadn't she said this man was safe?

What will Mr John do? Slightly couldn't see any way out – she couldn't think of anything to say to make things right. *If only I hadn't led him here!*

Then Mr John said something that took all of them by surprise.

'Miss Loch . . .' He cleared his throat and tried again. 'Miss Loch, may I just say that I think you are . . . you are . . . magnificent.'

Miss Loch's face was a picture. 'I . . . me . . . ?' She put a hand up to her dishevelled hair, looked down at her blood-stained blouse and bedraggled skirt and, ever so quietly, began to cry.

Chapter Eleven:

Slightly's Big Idea

'Oh!' said Slightly, horrified. Immediately every child in the place began to scold Mr John for making Miss cry and threatening her with jail, and if he thought they were going to let her be arrested he had another think coming.

And to all this Mr John paid no attention whatsoever.

Instead, he dropped down on his knees before Miss Loch, took her hands and shouted over the uproar, 'Oh don't, Miss Loch, I'm so sorry, I never meant . . . I'll do anything . . .'

'CHILDREN, BE QUIET!' bellowed Mr Malcolm suddenly and, for a wonder, they were.

Slightly took immediate advantage of the pause.

'Did you mean that?' she demanded of Mr John. 'When you said you'd do anything?'

'Anything,' he repeated fervently, still gazing at Miss Loch and clutching her hands.

'Well, you can not put her in prison for starters!'

That got his attention!

'*Prison?*' he exclaimed, turning to Slightly. 'For heroism like hers? Of course not! That is an appalling, an *outrageous* idea!'

Slightly jumped up. 'You mean, you're *not* going to have her arrested?' she cried in delight. The horrible weight on her heart lifted a little.

'How could you possibly think such a thing?' demanded Mr John.

'But . . . but . . .' blubbered Miss Loch, retrieving one of her hands from Mr John and waving it randomly around the tomb.

Mr John looked where she pointed and dismissed the lot.

'What? The things? We'll just put them back. In fact, now I think of it, you'd be doing the Museum an enormous favour if you didn't insist on being arrested. Imagine the embarrassment you'd save us! Think of the headlines: "Museum Trustees Totally Duped by Lovely Lady" . . . "Stealing from the Hunterian Proves to be Child's Play" . . . not to mention "Furnishing a Home? Forget Liberty's – Just Nick it from the Hunterian!" Oh, Miss Loch, please say I needn't arrest you!'

'Well, sir, since you ask so nicely,' said Miss Loch with a watery smile. 'We'll give the things back and . . . and say no more about it.'

'You're an angel – I mean, thank you so much.'

Slightly was having trouble controlling the grin on her face. Milly, however, had started to frown. 'Give back *everything*?' she said. 'Even my two wee toads?'

Mr John looked puzzled. 'Toads? I don't recall any amphibians on the list of stolen – that is to say, *mislaid* – items . . .'

'Now see there, Miss, he never even *noticed*!'

But Miss Loch shook her head. 'Everything, Milly,' she said firmly.

With a sigh, Milly drew a surprisingly clean handkerchief out of her pocket and unfolded it to reveal her 'toads' – a tiny sculpture of two animals, carved out of grey-green jade.

'Oh!' said Mr John. 'Those! Those are ancient jade lion dogs, from China. Qing Dynasty.'

But Milly didn't care. 'They've brought me luck, those toads,' she muttered.

'You could always go and visit them at the Museum,' suggested Slightly.

'Not the same,' she grumbled but, grudgingly, she held them out anyway.

Mr John took them and then drew the list of missing items from his coat pocket.

'If I might borrow your pencil, Miss Jones?' he said to Slightly and he drew a line through the words 'Lion Dogs, Qing Dynasty, jade' and wrote 'Recovered' in the margin.

'As soon as you are able to provide me with a somewhat less sepulchral address, Miss Milly,' he said solemnly, 'I will have your receipt sent, with the Museum's thanks.'

Milly looked up at him, her hands on her hips. 'You're daft,' she said.

And Mr John grinned, and turned back to Miss Loch.

Slightly had never seen him look so young! She heaved a big sigh and sat down on the edge of the babies' coffin. She was weary right through to her bones but the awful guilty feeling was almost gone. Mr Malcolm came over to join her, and she leaned against him gratefully.

'A receipt,' he murmured. 'Who but John would give a receipt to a thief!' Then, in response to Slightly's indignant look, he hurriedly added, 'Not that Milly is a thief, er, in a *bad* sense.'

'More of a borrower,' said Slightly.

'Of course,' said Mr Malcolm. Then, after a moment, he went on, 'He's right, though, about needing a new address. They can't stay here, none of them. Not with the winter coming on and all their things going back to the Hunterian. And,' here Mr Malcolm lowered his voice, 'I don't mean to alarm you, but there appear to be babies sleeping in this coffin.'

Slightly smiled at him. 'So they are,' she said. 'Nice and snug. Keeps out the drafts. As Milly says, they don't give nearly enough thought to caulking, these tomb builders. That's Rottenrow – he's teething – and Drygate in the middle, and that's Jane, though by rights her real name is North Canalbank.'

Mr Malcolm stared at her in utter amazement, but raised voices interrupted Slightly's enjoyment of it.

Miss Loch and Mr John were arguing.

It was about the children.

'I'll take them to an orphanage,' Mr John was saying.

This caused a great wail from the whole collection

of children, the smaller ones pressing closer to Miss Loch's skirts.

'No! We won't go!'

'Half of us ran *away* from the orphanage, mister!'

'The streets is better than that!'

'Miss, don't let him!'

'No orphanage,' said Miss Loch fiercely.

'But they can't stay here!' Mr John ran his hands through his hair in desperation. 'Please, children, stop crying! I can't *think*!'

'He's right and you're right,' said Slightly quietly to Mr Malcolm. 'They can't stay here. They need a proper house to live in. It'd have to be a big one, to take them all. You wouldn't want to split them up, would you? They're a family. And it'd have to be a pretty nice one too – they've got used to some very beautiful things about them.'

At this point, Rottenrow woke up and started to whinge again. Slightly picked him up almost absent-mindedly and began to walk up and down joggling him. She began to talk in time to the joggling. 'Now, I wonder where . . . would we find a place . . . that's very big . . . and going to waste . . .'

And then Slightly stopped short. She'd just had an idea that was so big, it very nearly made her brain explode.

It was my interfering got us into this mess in the first place, she thought. *Maybe my interfering can get us out of it now?*

Maybe it could.

She handed Rottenrow to Mr Malcolm.

She went up to the squabbling grown-ups, waved away the crying children, and began to talk . . .

Chapter Twelve:
Three Letters

It was a few months later, not long before Christmas in fact. In Glasgow, Jimmy, the ex-apprentice-resurrection-man, was working hard for his *other* uncle. Uncle Mungo was a butcher. He'd been saying for years, 'As soon as the lad's strong enough to carry half a dead cow on his back and chop the leg off a pig with one blow, then I'll take him on . . .'

Meanwhile, four hundred miles southeast, in London, some letters had arrived at Limpopo House.

Everyone was at home, in Granny

Tonic's kitchen – Granny, Slightly, Miss Forth, Mr Malcolm and Mr Thurgood and Mr Westerly, even Matthew Bone. He was teaching Miss Forth cockney rhyming slang and finding it quite a struggle. Not because Miss Forth was a poor pupil – far from it! – but because there were so many words he didn't feel it appropriate she should learn . . .

There was the postman's double knock, and Slightly skipped out to collect the post from the mat.

'Mr Malcolm, there's one for you *and it's from Glasgow*!' she cried as she raced back in. 'Oh, and Miss Forth, you have one as well,' she added.

Miss Forth took her letter and peered at the postmark. 'Ah!' she said with pleasure. 'My friend in Cambridge . . .' She opened the envelope and was soon absorbed in reading.

Slightly was trying hard not to show how desperate she was to hear what was in Mr Malcolm's letter. Her curiosity only got worse as the musician read his way carefully through the tightly written sheet, smiling to himself at this or that, murmuring 'Ah!' or 'Excellent!' from time to time . . . until Slightly couldn't bear it another minute.

'Mr *Malcolm*!' she blurted. 'What does he *say*?'

'That's very rude, Slightly,' Granny scolded. 'The contents of a private letter are not our business!'

'No, no,' said Mr Malcolm with a laugh. 'I shouldn't tease you, but it was such fun watching you all trying to act indifferent! The letter is for you as well. There, see? It begins *My dear Malcolm and all my friends at Limpopo House*. Let me read it to you. I won't bore you with the first paragraphs which are, as you might expect, about business but then he turns to the children – 'the ragtags' as he calls them. He says, *I have lost my watch and handkerchief so many times that it has become a standing joke – no matter how alert I try to be, there is always one set of little fingers that gets past my guard. They work together, the little devils, and distract my attention in the most cunning ways . . . I am working out a programme of education which I hope will soon keep them too busy to rob me! Music, you will be pleased to hear, is to be part of the curriculum. However I have no plans to unearth Father's old cane. I think we know well enough that that is not the way to learn!*' Mr Malcolm paused and looked round at his friends. 'My brother is a fine man,' he said. 'He really is.'

There was a murmur of agreement and Slightly was glad to think no child would ever walk the halls like an unhappy ghost again.

'But what about Miss Loch?' she asked Slightly eagerly. 'What does he say about Miss Loch?'

Mr Gentler chuckled and read out, '*You will be*

wondering how things are between me and Miss Loch, "my happiness from the grave". Well, progress is slow. Even though I have moved her entire tribe into the Gentler mansion, I believe she is still testing me, to see if my affection for the children is genuine, or merely a way of winning her heart. But, as you know, I am a patient man and, quite aside from a growing liking for the ragtags (even the ones that remind me of your friend Master Bone!) . . .'

'Oi!' exclaimed Matthew, but nobody paid any attention.

'. . . *I'm enjoying the business of turning the house you and I grew up in into a proper home. I think, left to her own devices, my Katrine would simply have made a gypsy nest for them all with the furnishings as they are – not unlike their home in the tomb. I intend them to have something more appropriate. Something permanent. I suspect I don't need to tell you that Mrs Mull is supremely happy.* And then he adds . . . *P.S. Enclosed please find something that should please Miss Jones.*' Mr Malcolm paused to pull another, smaller piece of paper out of the envelope and handed it to Slightly.

It was quite crumpled and there was an inky thumbprint clearly visible by the fold. Slightly frowned, puzzled, but as soon as she opened the paper, the frown turned into a delighted smile.

'It's from Milly!' she cried. 'She's learning to write!'

It was not a letter in the usual sense, since it consisted only of the alphabet, painstakingly copied out, with many a smudge and wobble. But the picture drawn in the space beneath communicated volumes! With a big grin, Slightly held it up for the others to see. The figures were simply drawn but there was no doubt in anybody's mind who they were meant to be.

'See?' she said. 'It's Miss Loch and Mr John holding hands, in front of Glasgow Cathedral – look, you can even see a hill behind with some tombs – she's included the Necropolis! Well, he has Milly's blessing, at any rate!'

'And all ours as well, when the time comes!' said Granny.

Mr Westerly and Mr Thurgood nodded agreement. Mr Malcolm's smile was beatific as he began to hum the tune from Mendelssohn's *Wedding March*. Matthew Bone pulled a face at such sentimentality. On the other hand, Slightly expected to hear a great upswelling of twittered emotion from Miss Forth. But Miss Forth said nothing!

Miss Forth wasn't listening. She was engrossed in her own letter.

'Oh, how strange!' she murmured. 'How very *mysterious* . . . Oh, goodness!'

Immediately Slightly felt her ears begin to prick.

'Mysterious?' she said. 'What's mysterious?'

Miss Forth looked up and blushed as she realised that everyone was staring at her.

'Well, but it really is most out of the ordinary!' she exclaimed.

'What is, Miss Forth?' asked Granny patiently.

'This!' said Miss Forth, laying her letter down on the kitchen table and pointing at it dramatically.

'What does it say?' cried Slightly.

And Miss Forth told them what was in the letter from her friend in Cambridge. It was, indeed, an out-of-the-ordinary tale, involving a mysterious curse, an ancient necklace, Egyptian mummies, smashed artefacts, unanswered questions . . . and bicycles.

'My friend doesn't know *what* to do!' she finished.

It sounded *wonderful*!

Granny took one look at Slightly's shining eyes and threw up her hands in defeat.

With a huge grin on her face, the young detective turned to Miss Forth.

'Tell her to do nothing!' said Slightly Jones. 'Tell her . . . we'll take the case!'

TO BE CONTINUED IN
The Case of the Cambridge Mummy

Discover some fascinating facts about Victorian Glasgow . . .

Did you know . . .

. . . that it wasn't just Victorian London that had terrible fogs?

All the big cities in Victorian Britain had real problems with what we now call smog. In his report in 1880, R. Russell said of London:

In winter more than a million chimneys breathe forth simultaneously smoke, soot, sulphurous acid, vapour of water, and carbonic acid gas, and the whole town fumes like a vast crater, at the bottom of which its unhappy citizens must creep and live as best they can . . .

It was like that in Glasgow too. Deaths and illness from chest infections and breathing problems increased enormously whenever there was fog. People were run over by horses and carriages, and hundreds of thefts were reported. And it wasn't just in Victorian times – yellow, smelly, choking fogs went on being a menace to British city dwellers well into the twentieth century.

... that the City of the Dead was designed by a competition?

In 1831 a competition was launched to find the best design for Glasgow's new Necropolis (the first garden cemetery in Scotland). The prizes ranged from £10 to £50. David Bryce of Edinburgh came first and his brother, John Bryce of Glasgow, came second, which may have caused a bit of family tension! But in the end, the cemetery was designed from a combination of all the good things from the top five entries.

... how to read a Victorian tombstone?

It's easy enough to read the names and inscriptions when they're in English, but the Victorians also used symbols on their gravestones – it was like a code that everybody understood. Here are some of the images they used and their meanings:

immortality

a young death

hope **a younger person's death** **an older person's death**

entrance from this world to the next **time flies** **grief**

Even the dates aren't always easy for us to read. Roman numerals were often used. Using the chart below, can you translate this date? MDCCCLXXXVI

M = 1000 D = 500 C = 100
L = 50 X = 10 V = 5 I = 1

Next time you get a chance to visit a Victorian cemetery, see if you can read what the symbols mean.

Glasgow Quiz

Test your knowledge of Victorian and modern-day Glasgow with these questions . . .

If you got on the Glasgow Subway the day after it opened in 1896, how long would it take you to go right round the system?

Mr Malcolm Gentler had good reason to boast about the Glasgow Subway. It was the third underground railway ever to be built, after London and Budapest. But it was the first in the world to solve the problem of what to do with all the steam and smoke and soot from the train engines that was always dirtying and choking the passengers!

By having a separate, stationary steam engine and seven-mile-long cables, the Glasgow trains were pulled round the inner and outer circle in a smoke-free environment. Well, as long as you sat in the front carriage (the one with the red leather seats) because passengers were allowed to smoke in the back carriage – the one with brown leather seats. I guess they didn't want the beautiful red ones dirtied!

If you visit the Hunterian Museum today, can you find the following?

- Milly's lucky wee toads, otherwise known as the Jade Lion Dogs
- Dr Joseph Lister's carbolic spraying machine
- The Rembrandt painting *The Entombment*
- An eye in a bottle
- A drawing of an amazingly tall giraffe on an ancient Chinese map of the world

To find the answers to these questions and learn more about her other books, visit the author's website:

www.joanlennon.co.uk

Congratulations to Katherine Jarvis, age 10, of Broughty Ferry, the winner of the Slightly Jones Art-y-fact Drawing Competition. The challenge was to invent an object that could have been stolen from the Hunterian Museum by the mysterious thieves. Katherine's object was a gold Celtic brooch with a jade rabbit on it, found in North Cornwall and possibly worn by Emma of Normandy, wife of King Canute. Intriguing! To see her winning entry, go to Slightly's own website: **www.slightlyjones.co.uk**. Well done, Katherine!

COMING SOON

A SLIGHTLY JONES MYSTERY

The Case of the Cambridge Mummy

An ancient curse has been let loose in cold wintry Cambridge. Priceless artefacts are found, mysteriously crushed into dust at the Fitzwilliam Museum – long-dead Egyptian queens stalk the corridors of Girton College – and what do bicycles and bloomers have to do with it all?

Slightly Jones is faced with her most bewildering case yet – and her most ruthless opponents. Can she find the answer in time, or will it be a bleak mid-winter for everyone?